Snow Stuck

A SUMMERS IN CHRISTMAS NOVEL

ELLE RIVERS

Cover Design by Summer Grove

Edited by Kasey Kubica, Basic Behemoth Edits

Proofread by Mae Peredo, Wildwood Author Services

❀ Created with Vellum

A NOTE FROM ELLE

This novel contains scenes some might find upsetting. In this book, a character sleeps with someone older while eighteen. A member of the family has very strong opinions about it. Their intention is to be protective, but it comes across as sexist in some scenes. Also, parental abandonment is discussed and happens to a character off-page.

I do not consider this novel to be darker than any of my other works, but if you come across a potential trigger not mentioned here, please email me at elle@ellerivers.com.

For anyone who feels like their shine has been dulled.
Find the person who brings out the best in you.

PROLOGUE

STELLA

THE HOT CHOCOLATE in my hands was some of the best I'd ever had.

If I could have somehow captured the taste of this perfect mix of cocoa and sugar with a hint of peppermint in a photo, I would. I didn't know whose recipe this was, but it was made from scratch and possibly with nectar from the gods.

Unfortunately for me, all I could do was snap a picture of the cup in my hand. I would have to remember everything else myself.

I'd had bad hot chocolate from many places. Whether it was premade powdered mix or made only with water and cocoa powder, the disappointment of a bad drink carried over into whatever would happen next. This incredible one was hopefully the first of many things going my way.

I was already in a good mood when one of my old

high school friends invited me to this party. The Christmas season always added some pep to my step, but this year had been especially good.

Not only had my first semester of college ended with me getting As and Bs in all my classes, but I'd also changed roommates from the horrible school-assigned one to my best friend, Winnie. Everything was in order and I only had one goal for this party.

Tonight, I would lose my virginity. Winnie was also attempting the same thing, but she had a higher chance considering she was a total knockout with her light brown skin and long braids. While she hadn't dated once in high school, she had plenty of opportunities in places that I didn't.

We could have done it while on campus, but both of us had been far too busy trying to stay afloat with our workloads. But we could have the last week of school if we wanted to.

But I had my sights set on someone *not* at college.

And he was my brother's best friend.

My eye had been on Alden Canes ever since I discovered that the opposite sex was attractive, but he always kept me at a frustrating arm's-length distance. For a while, I got it. I was the annoying little sister of his best friend and he was four years older.

But now, I was an adult, and my plan was in motion.

I'd seen him looking at me when he thought I wouldn't notice, especially as I'd continued to grow curves over the years. Some would say I was overweight, but I worked hard to love my body.

And when I wore low-cut shirts, I *swear* I had caught Alden looking twice and then averting his eyes. I could never ask him about it because he was *always* with my older brother, Nick.

But tonight, Nick was in the middle of a shift at his cashier job. Alden, on the other hand, was free and had been invited to the party by the host, who Alden knew through their older brother. All manner of students from freshmen year to senior were present, which meant Alden wasn't singled out as the oldest one.

And when he arrived, I'd find him.

I was mingling by the Christmas tree, admiring the house the party was in. It was tastefully decorated, save for the makeshift beer pong table and Walmart snacks thrown on every surface. To add to my memories of this potentially perfect night, I took a few photos of the gorgeous tree beside me.

I was always taking pictures like this. One day I might be able to make it my full-time job, even though the degree I was currently working toward was in a different field.

There was no telling where I would end up, but there was one thing I was willing to guarantee.

My crush on Alden was never going to change.

I could feel it the second he walked in at eight on the dot. I abandoned my photos to watch him. His eyes perused the crowd and he waved at some of the people he knew.

My brother's best friend had one of those faces you couldn't help but stare at. His angular jaw and teakwood eyes were what pulled most people in. Sometimes it was the way his raven-colored hair was always styled back on his head. But for me, it was the way he smiled.

It was a rare concept these days. Alden didn't have a great homelife, especially after his mom died a decade ago. It got worse recently when his father stopped talking to him after marrying an eighteen-year-old girl.

Alden told his father it was wrong, and his father replied that he was going to do what he wanted and to stay away from him if he was going to criticize. They'd never had a great relationship, but this was the final nail in the coffin.

He'd always spent time with us as a kid, but after, he became a real part of the family—a staple at every event.

I was sure Nick wanted me to see him in a brotherly way, but my crush only grew. Especially once he started smiling again.

It took about six months to crack his sad exterior, but he finally let loose when Nick and I were screaming at each other over Mario Kart. We'd traded increasingly petty insults until Alden was laughing. When we saw that, all of the fight left us, and we celebrated him coming back out of his shell.

I was awarded one of these rare smiles when Alden's

eyes locked with mine, and my heart skipped a beat as he approached me.

"Hey," he said. "I'm surprised you're not with your partner in crime."

"Oh, Winnie? She's on the couch having the time of her life."

I pointed to the other room, and Alden's eyebrows reached his hairline when he caught her lip-locked with Kadie Henry, the cheerleader of her dreams. This was the most I'd seen her touch anyone since she usually kept her distance, but nothing could stop her when she was determined.

"Seems like she's having fun."

"You know Winnie. She's always having fun."

"Except when she's around Nick."

"Not everyone can like my brother," I replied. "I barely like him some days."

His eyes slid back over to me and I saw him do his familiar double take. The first thing he glanced at was my teal sweater showing off my boobs. He quickly looked away, but his eyes returned, this time traveling over the rest of me. I'd done my makeup perfectly and my cheeks glistened in the low lights of the party.

"Like my sweater?" I asked. "I got it from Target this week. I wanted something that screamed more Christmas, but they were out of red."

"Red isn't your best color."

"Then what is?"

He looked away and vaguely gestured at the top I was wearing.

A compliment?

Yes.

I waited for him to say something, or worse, walk back what he had just said. He stayed silent.

"Forget how to talk?" I asked demurely.

"H-how is school going? Shouldn't you be studying?"

"Studying for what? It's Christmas break."

"Already?"

"College lets out earlier, remember?"

"Right," he said, rubbing the side of his neck. "You're already in college."

"You helped me move in."

"It's still hard to believe you're mostly out on your own. How's campus life?"

"It's . . . something. I had a bad roommate this semester but I'll have Winnie in the next one. I forced our RA to approve moving me."

"Forced?"

"More like annoyed into submission. Either way, next semester will be way easier. But for now, I get to celebrate my favorite holiday of the year with company."

"Whose?"

I tapped my finger on my chin, scanning all of the people around me. "I *could* go get hit on by the football team." That was a bluff. I doubted any of them would want me around. Alden's face darkened anyway. "Or hang out with you."

"I think I prefer the second thing."

I was *killing* it.

"Then I guess I'll remain here." I smiled. "I'm a legal adult, so I can make whatever decision I want."

"I never asked you—does it feel different?"

"Only when the gods of consent came down and told me I could do what I want."

Alden rolled his eyes, but one corner of his mouth quirked up. "Yeah, yeah. You didn't even see the real gods anyway. You can't drink."

I scrunched my nose. "Not that I want to. But no, it doesn't feel different to me. Why do you ask? Do I *look* different?"

"N-no." He said it a little too slowly.

"Come on. You can admit it."

The muscles in his neck tightened.

This conversation was charged in ways none of our previous ones had been. Even when we were both minors, I was too awkward, and he was too close to Nick to look twice at me.

But now it was just the two of us and anything could happen.

"You look like you're ready for a good night." He rubbed the back of his neck, looking away. "If you wanted to go hang out with the jocks, you could. I won't tell anyone."

My eyes stayed on him. "I'm good right here." I tilted my head, the way Winnie told me looked best, and

Alden's gaze lingered on my neck for a second longer than usual.

"Your hair is curled today," he said.

"I figured this was a special occasion. Do you like it?"

"It looks nice." He said it lowly, in a voice I'd never heard before.

"I'm not used to it like this." I swished it over my shoulder and his eyes followed the movement. "But maybe I'll curl it more often."

I waited for the moment that he would look away and pretend he never saw it. But his eyes stayed on me, and I would bask in every second of it.

I took a chance and stepped closer. In his space, I could see the stubble on his jaw and his dark-brown eyes. Christmas lights illuminated him, giving him an ethereal glow.

"You should try some of this." I held up my cup of hot chocolate. "It's delicious."

His hand curled around mine for one second as he grabbed the drink. "Is this where you tell me it's spiked?"

"Not this time. It's just delicious chocolate and milk."

He took a sip from the cup, mouth exactly where mine had been. I bit my lip as I watched him closely.

"It's good."

"You have a little on your—" I leaned forward to wipe it from his bottom lip, bringing us closer. His eyes closed as I grazed my thumb over his mouth and I let it linger for a few seconds longer.

My hand trailed to his shoulder. I waited for him to

step away and steer the conversation back to something casual.

He did not do that.

I should have gotten him away from Nick *much* sooner. This was not as difficult as I thought it would be.

My fingers pressed into the hard muscle. "You seem stressed."

"Yeah, my finals weren't easy this time, which makes no sense since I'm not in one of the fancy schools like you are. Plus, I have the added pressure of figuring out what the hell to do with my life when I graduate."

"That sounds like a lot. Need to forget about it for a bit?"

"I . . . I'm not sure how."

"I *hear* that getting lost in someone else is great stress relief."

"Have anyone in mind?"

"I do, actually. She's got long hair and green eyes. Five foot six and in front of you."

He took a shaky breath. "We shouldn't."

"Why not? I think we'd *both* enjoy it."

"But Nick . . ."

I put my finger on his lips. "Do me a favor and don't mention my brother right now."

His throat worked again when my hand was on his face. "I think . . . I think I could go for some stress relief."

A smile curled on my lips. "That's exactly what I was hoping you would say."

* * *

ALDEN'S TRUCK had a surprisingly big back seat. If it were any other day, I would have wondered how it comfortably held my wide hips despite looking tiny.

But his lips were on mine, so I didn't have very many thoughts.

Now that I had his attention, I didn't waste a second. Stopping to go somewhere more private wasn't even on my mind because I didn't want to let Alden think too much about this.

I wanted him. And he wanted me, but sometimes his brain made things hard. If I could prove to him just how good this could be, then he would see that we could work together.

He was an incredible kisser—nothing like the boy I'd made out with at the library after school a few years ago. That had been sloppy and forgettable.

But *this*? This was everything. His lips were fire, moving at a pace that I wasn't used to. I opened myself to him and his tongue dipped into my mouth, letting his taste mix with mine.

I groaned as he pressed his whole body against me. I finally got to run my hands along his muscular shoulders, a dream I didn't ever think would come to fruition.

His hand drifted under my sweater to my lower back. No man had ever touched me there before, and my skin erupted in gooseflesh.

Alden's hold on me was tight, but it kept me from

floating away in my mind. I tightened my hands on his shirt, happy this was real instead of a dream this time.

His other hand was on my hip, fingers right at the band of my leggings. I waited for far too long before pulling away.

"Take them off," I said. "My leggings, I mean."

His hand on my hip tightened. "You sure?"

"So sure. More sure than anything else."

We had to wiggle around to get them off, but I felt more alive once the cool air hit me. Alden's eyes roamed over my hips, taking in every inch of me. He licked his lips and his hand cupped my ass.

"Sweater now," I said between gasps.

He followed orders, and his gaze was on my see-through lace bra once my top was off. "Fuck," he said breathlessly.

When his lips closed over mine again, Alden's hand cupped my waiting breast. The lace rubbed against my sensitive skin and my nipples were begging for attention.

I reached out to unlatch my bra, revealing my entire top half to him.

His eyes hovered on my breasts for only a beat before he pulled off his pants, showing me the first real-life cock I'd ever seen.

I'd prepped myself for this in the privacy of my room, but seeing it in the flesh and knowing where I wanted it sent chills down my spine. Alden's mouth claimed mine again, and I could feel his hardness against my leg. Our kisses grew heavier and his breathing stuttered when I sunk my teeth into his lip.

He pulled away and I had a second to catch my breath before he kissed my cheek and my neck. He returned the bite right where my neck met my collarbone and I let out a broken gasp.

"Touch me." My core was dying for attention.

"Are you—"

"Yes," I said. "I'm very sure. Now, *please* touch me."

"So polite," he said with a devious grin.

His hand trailed my already wet pussy, fingers meeting the folds where I needed him. My head dropped back, eyes fluttering closed.

I couldn't believe this was happening. I couldn't believe Alden Canes was doing what I'd asked of him.

The feeling of pressure on my most sensitive areas made me see stars. His fingers circled, caressed, and tortured my clit as I jerked my hips into his hand.

His breaths were hot in my ear, and while this felt good, I also knew my body would need a while to warm up.

"We can focus on you if you want to." I knew some guys didn't want to wait for the woman to orgasm, and while I thought it was bullshit, I'd give Alden some grace because I liked him so much.

"Take all the time you need, baby," he whispered into my ear. "I've got all night."

His fingers moved in the perfect way and I moaned.

Not only was he good at this, but he was patient too. What a turn-on.

I moved my hips against his hand, giving myself the pleasure I needed. The heat in my body built, ready to tumble over the edge, but it took longer than if it were just me. He'd told me to take all the time I needed, so I did. I moved how I needed to, jerking my hips to chase the feeling I fiercely craved.

But then I felt his hard cock against my leg again and my mind flashed to what that was going to feel like when he fucked me.

I *needed* it. I couldn't wait for it.

The mental image alone was enough to send me tumbling over the edge. I gasped and leaned into him as pleasure hit every nerve in my body.

I was out of breath when the sensation finally ebbed, but the second it was over, I was ready for more.

"Keep going," I said. "I need another one."

"I'd be happy to, but what if I gave you my mouth this time?" he asked.

"Yes. But there isn't room."

He moved and opened the door. It wasn't cold, even for December, but I doubted that my body would even feel it if it were.

"I'll kneel on the ground if it means I get to taste you. Come here."

"But what if people see?"

"No one will bother coming this far down the street. It's just us here."

That was all the convincing I needed. I'd probably do anything if it came out of Alden's mouth. I moved to the edge of the seat, and his mouth clamped down on my desperate pussy. I'd imagined what this could feel like, but this was otherworldly.

I ran my fingers through his hair, keeping him close to me. My body sang as he ran his tongue around my clit, shooting me toward another perfect release.

Yet, I wanted one other thing.

"Finger fuck me," I said between gasps. "Please."

"I didn't know you had such a dirty mouth." I looked down to see a smile on his lips.

"There's a lot you don't know, and you won't if you don't make me come again."

"Yes, ma'am," he said. I didn't know if he liked this side of me, but I didn't have it in me to question myself. His finger entered me slowly.

This was the first time someone else had done this. My body clenched around him, but not out of fear, out of pleasure. I'd spent countless nights wishing he was the one inside of me, and now I had everything I wanted.

Alden's finger hooked, finding a spot inside that I never could. I let out a gasp and arched into him.

His mouth came down on my clit again, sucking gently. His finger, only slightly curved now, pulled in and out of me, and my pussy gripped it with every movement.

I wanted that to be his cock so badly. The silicone ones stashed under my bed weren't enough.

But I was busy feeling like I was floating. He played me like a fiddle, and I wanted to remember every second of it. My breaths quickened as every nerve ending lit on fire.

"That's it," he said, "I want to feel it."

I came again, this sensation sharper than the last. My body was a million fireworks exploding in a perfect symphony.

"Very good," he said just as my senses came back to me. For a moment, I wasn't able to formulate a response. I didn't even know where I *was*—only that my orgasm had been mind-blowing.

He stood and I eyed his cock, which was wet with anticipation.

"Please fuck me," I said. "Please fuck me in the back seat of your truck."

"Gladly," he said lowly. He grabbed a condom from his center console and then hovered over me.

The head of his cock swirled at my opening, and I closed my eyes so I could feel every second of it. The anticipation was killing me.

He pressed in, just a touch, pushing against my inner walls. My breathing stuttered. *Finally.* This was going to happen.

He pulled out and I made a pitiful noise. "Why'd you pull away?"

"Because this is . . . Look at me," he said, and I followed his instructions. "Is this what you want?"

"Yes," I said breathlessly. "A million times yes. I would

tattoo it on my forehead if I could." He bit his lip, still unconvinced, but I put a hand on his chest. "Alden, I want this. You can *feel* how much I do."

It helped. Some of the concern left his face, and I felt that hardness press in again, but this time, he slid in an inch.

"More," I said. "Give me more."

"I don't want to hurt you," he said through gritted teeth.

"You won't. I want all of you. Come on, Alden. Fuck me."

This time, he didn't stop. He pushed and slipped through my wetness, seating himself all of the way in.

I gasped. Nothing could have prepared me for how *close* he was, how his pelvis touched mine, how he invaded me in a way no one else had.

And the way that this felt *intimate*.

"Fuck," he muttered, his jaw tight.

"Yeah, that's the right word."

"I don't know if I can be gentle."

"I don't want gentle," I said. "Ruin me for other men. I dare you."

And his control snapped like a taut string. His hands gripped my hips like a vise and he slammed into me all the way to the hilt.

I'd always wanted sex because I liked orgasms, but this was more. This felt like a promise. As he did it over and over again, I saw stars.

"Yes," I said. "That's what I'm talking about."

I knew I would be sore, but the slight pain somehow added to the pleasure. He was inside of me, all of him, and I knew there was no greater Christmas present than this.

Alden pulled out of me one last time, and I was ready for his relentless assault to continue, but instead, he rolled me over.

"Don't want to see my face?" I half joked.

"I love your face, but I want to see your ass move as I fuck you." His hand gripped my hips from a new angle. "And I want you to come again."

"I don't think I can from just this," I said.

"Touch yourself."

I wanted to pipe up and tell him that there was no way this would feel as good as he was making it out to be, but I also wanted him inside of me again, so I did as I was told.

And I was immediately rewarded. This time, when his cock entered me, it was different. It felt tighter, with an addictive burn. Once he was all the way in, I realized he was hitting that spot inside of me at this angle.

I snaked my arm down, pressing my fingers into my own wet flesh. His hips pumped into me, moving mine with every relentless thrust. The movement made me see stars and I let out a gasping breath.

"That's right. I can hear it in your breath. It feels good."

I didn't even have words. This was better than anything I'd ever felt before. My body was in the clouds from this. My hand pressed in tighter and I could feel myself building once again.

"I'm . . . I'm gonna come."

"Good," he said, speeding up.

I erupted, heat traveling from where he was inside of me all the way to my belly and toes. I felt everything release in a wave, taking me with it.

"Alden, yes," I said. It didn't stop. As long as he was moving, I was riding the wave. My pussy clenched him as his movements became erratic.

"You feel too fucking good," he said. "Better than I imagined. Oh, *fuck*."

His hips slammed into me one last time before I could feel his cock pulsing.

As I lay there, gasping for breath, I knew that I would be fucking this man again. I would feel this *again*. I was making it happen.

"I didn't hurt you, did I?"

"No," I said. "That was fucking amazing."

"Good," he replied. "Let's clean up."

"I want to sleep for a day straight." I was still loopy from the high I was coming down from.

"Whatever you want, baby. Whatever you want."

ALDEN

I was driving Stella to her house when one thought hit me.

She's the same age as Dad's new wife.

Any lingering pleasure evaporated.

I tried not to think of my dad much, especially since he was content to live his life and forget about me, but every now and then, the thoughts slipped in.

The day I found out, I was sick to my stomach. She had been sitting at the living room table, and my first thought was that she was someone Dad was trying to set *me* up with, but then she flashed her ring and I found out the truth.

Later, I heard from one of his friends that he'd been with her *before* she was eighteen, and it was the final straw in our already bad relationship.

I wasn't my dad. That much I knew. I was half his age and a better person.

But the *thought* made me rethink my choices. I'd made a promise never to touch my best friend's little sister while she was underage and kept true to that. It didn't matter that I meshed better with her than anyone else. It didn't matter that I found her gorgeous for way too long.

I wasn't going there.

But she was in that damn low-cut sweater, and I couldn't stop myself.

I'd been lost in lust, but the way I talked to her was nothing like the friendship we'd fostered over the years. I wanted to be like a brother to her, but the way my mind betrayed me was one of the reasons I was up at night.

And now, *this* would stick with me—in more ways than one. I could already tell I wanted her again, even though I shouldn't. Sure, there wasn't technically anything wrong with this, but I had a feeling Nick wouldn't be thrilled.

While he would never tell her *not* to date anyone, he certainly made it known when he didn't think someone was good enough for her. And I had a feeling he would have the same opinion about me.

I could lie, but I refused to do that to him. He was my best friend, always there for me when the only family I had walked away. I'd kept my growing attraction to Stella to myself because I knew he was protective over her.

The fact that I slept with her when she hadn't even been eighteen for six months didn't make me look good.

It wasn't illegal, even if she hadn't been eighteen, because the gap had to be *over* four years in Tennessee, and we were under that by a month.

But it still felt *wrong*.

She didn't feel wrong, though. The sex had been the best of my life. It was wild in a way I could have only imagined, and I would love to do it again. I'd noticed her as she grew up, but she was always too young.

She was *still* too young, but I could only hope I wouldn't get in too much trouble with Nick over it.

"I'm gonna go to my room," Stella said as we pulled in. Her smile was catlike. "You can join me."

"I should probably catch up with Nick first," I said. "Especially since he's home from work."

"Okay." She stood on tiptoes and pressed a kiss on my cheek. "I'll be waiting."

Even with my guilt, my body reacted to her. God, I wanted this.

I shouldn't.

I waited until Stella was in her room and let out a long breath of air.

Time to face the music.

Nick was in his room, watching TV after a long day. He'd been working extra to save up for a place he and I could share once we both graduated next semester. I wasn't sure what I wanted to do with my life after college, and I needed a place to live while I figured it out.

My job at a local outdoor store paid three-quarters of the posted rent for most apartment complexes around here, but it wasn't enough. Nick didn't have to offer to live with me at all since Mr. and Mrs. Summers would let him continue living at home, but I was more than grateful that he did.

"Hey," Nick said. "How was the party?"

"Fun." I cleared my throat. "Stella was there."

He frowned. "She was? She isn't the partying type. Who invited her?"

"I didn't ask."

"Was there alcohol?"

"Yes, but she didn't have any. She was sober the whole time."

"Good," he said, giving me a half smile. "She's not like me, at least. I don't think Mom and Dad could have handled that. Neither could I, now that I think about it."

Nick and Stella couldn't be more different. He got into as much trouble as he could. She stuck to the rules.

Nick wasn't always this protective over his sister, but she was bullied in middle school to the point that she stopped eating for way too long. When we found out about it, he and I came to her defense. Then she met Winnie and everything changed.

I needed to get this over with. "She was with someone, though."

"Who?" His eyes narrowed and I instantly filled with dread.

"Me."

"Oh, so you made sure she didn't do anything dumb?"

"Uh, mostly. But I mean when I was *with* her, I mean in a . . . more than friends way."

Nick froze, and when his eyes moved to me, they were like ice. "You didn't."

"I did."

"Are you fucking serious?"

I took a step back. His voice was low, more like a growl than anything else.

The only time he'd ever talked like this was when he found the kids who had upset Stella when she was in middle school. I never thought he would turn it around on *me*, even if I'd been with her.

"Yeah, I am."

That was the wrong thing to say. He stood. "Do you know how fucking gross that is?"

"I don't know about *gross*—"

"Alden, you knew her when she was a kid. She's *four* years younger than you."

"Weren't we also kids?"

"Older kids!" he snapped. "What the hell were you thinking going after her?"

"I didn't go after her at all! I said hello."

He crossed his arms. "Then how the hell did you end up with her?"

I closed my eyes. I don't even know how we'd ended up in the back of my truck. Most of our conversation was drowned out by that damn teal sweater she'd been wearing. "Things just ended up that way."

"Just ended up that way?" he asked. "Try again."

"I don't . . . I'm telling you the truth. What else do you want from me?"

"For you to have walked away from my little sister, Alden."

"I didn't just use her or anything. I *like* her."

"She's my *sister*. You don't feel anything for her. Besides, she's too young to know better."

"Stella is an adult," I reminded him.

"Fuck off," he snapped, his glare piercing. "Isn't that what your dad said about his new wife?"

Fuck. He had. All the regret hit me again. I promised never to sound like my dad or date anyone younger than me.

But there was one defense I had.

"It's only four years."

"So, I guess you're not going to see sense then." He

shook his head. "I need to do the same thing you did to your dad."

"Wh-what?"

"I'm not staying friends with a guy who takes advantage of my sister."

"I didn't mean to take advantage of her, I just—"

"You did."

"She consented."

"I don't care! God, Alden, *why* would I want my best friend crawling around her? I thought you were better." He looked away. "Guess I thought wrong. Get out."

Panic hit me—the same panic as when Dad left with his new wife. The same panic as when I found out Mom was gone and wouldn't be coming home.

I couldn't be left by one more person. The only person who had stuck around was Nick, and through him, I knew the Summers—the only family I had left. If I ruined things with him then I ruined things with them all.

"I'm sorry," I rushed to say.

"It's too late for that."

"Let me fix this."

"Fix it?"

"Yes. I'll do whatever you want me to do."

I was half convinced he would tell me to leave anyway, but instead, he looked just as pained as I did. I could only hope that he didn't want to hate me as much as I didn't want to hate him.

I gave him time, praying that he could think of something.

"Break it off with her," he finally said. "And never look at her again."

"Not even be friends with her?"

I couldn't imagine my life without Stella in it. Even when we were kids, she made me as happy as Nick did.

"Can you stay away from her if you're friends with her?"

I wanted to say yes. It would have been easier if I could.

But I knew the truth. "I don't know if I can."

"Then leave her alone."

My head hung heavy. I was keeping Nick but losing Stella. And it *hurt*.

"Don't try to make me feel bad," he said. "You should have never touched her."

"I know," I replied. "I'll keep my distance."

He gave me a stiff nod and looked away. It was a clear dismissal, and I left his room without another word.

Down the hall, Stella's door stood innocently. She'd invited me to spend time with her, but I knew I wouldn't take her up on that. If I were smart, I'd march in there and tell her we could never do this again.

Even the thought made me feel like the biggest asshole in the world. I didn't *want* to break it off with her. I didn't want to hurt her.

Emotion was taking over, filling me with a despair that had no outlet. I couldn't tell her about this. She didn't get why Nick was overprotective, and I couldn't hide it from her if I tried. Nick wanted nothing to do with me, and I had no one else.

So, I ran.

Ran to the quiet of a nearby park, where I sat in my truck and regretted all of the choices I'd made that night.

Silence was my only companion for hours, and eventually, I calmed down enough to send a text.

ALDEN

> This can't happen again. I'm sorry, but we won't work out.

I hated myself for it. I wished I could take it back the moment I hit send.

But I couldn't lose my best friend. I couldn't take one more person walking away.

It didn't mean it was easier to be the one *pushing* someone away, though.

ONE

STELLA

I TOOK another sip of my drink, cringing at the bitter taste. My boyfriend, Reed, made this hot chocolate, and like most of the things he concocted, it was disgusting.

It was possible that the only ingredients were water and cocoa powder since he didn't believe in using sugar.

I stood in the corner of his high-rise apartment, wearing heels that dug into my feet. Reed asked me to dress up for this in the same muted colors he'd been begging me to wear since last year. This time it was a mauve that high-school me wouldn't have been caught dead in.

He'd told me it was because there would be a lot of photos, and it was best not to outshine his mother, Patricia, who was in a tight, candy-red dress. But I wouldn't be *in* the photos, considering I was also the photographer of the evening.

I didn't think I would celebrate Christmas with his

family by working, but they insisted I take their portraits. Instead of mingling, I'd been running around getting shots of everyone.

Reed said it was because I was good at my job, but I knew it was because he wanted me to be busy. Last Christmas, I'd been too boisterous after having spiked hot chocolate. Patricia *still* referred to me as the girl with the guffaw.

After that, I learned to stay quiet. But doing so burned me in a way I wasn't used to. There was a quiet resentment at Reed and Patricia that I couldn't fight. And it was getting harder to ignore.

Winnie told me I shouldn't have to change at all. I wanted to agree with her, but after a line of men telling me they either didn't feel a spark or that I wasn't their type, landing Reed felt like a win. He was my first serious adult relationship. I wanted this to work.

So here I was, in a mauve dress, keeping my mouth shut.

I fucking hated it.

I felt as bitter as the hot chocolate in my hand, but today, I had to put on a brave face since all of his family was here. This was the one night they were in the city before they went to the Florida Keys for Christmas. Reed invited me on the trip, but I turned him down, knowing I couldn't be away from my family for the holiday.

He'd planned this party instead. It said a lot that I was hoping that he would tell me he was going to the Keys instead of staying with me in town.

If he did, I didn't have to bring him to my own family's holiday party. He'd only met them once, and it was at Christmas last year. If anyone in my circle saw what I was wearing, they'd do the dumping for me.

I knew what was happening here. This relationship, like all of my others, wouldn't work. I'd have to break it to him soon.

Maybe I should say it was the hot chocolate. The abysmal drink was enough to break *anyone* up.

I checked my watch. If he didn't say he was going with his family, maybe I would tell him tonight that he *should* go to the Keys and I'd stay here.

I'd pack up my stuff and be gone by the time he got back.

"There you are!" Reed's sister, Lacy, said, popping up in front of me with a smile on her face. "I've been looking for you."

"Looking for me? Really?" I asked. Lacy rarely talked to me and chose to whisper in the corner with Patricia at every family gathering.

"Yes, duh. I need to do a gender reveal soon and you're my favorite photographer." She ran a hand over her rounded stomach.

That was when it hit me. Lacy wasn't here to be nice. She was here because she wanted something from me.

"Um, I'm not sure if a family dinner is the place to network."

"You're working anyway." She laughed as if this were

something I *wanted* to do. "Besides, I have the best idea. A baseball reveal at a local park."

"Which one?"

"Redstone Falls south of Nashville."

Nope. That was not my territory.

"I don't work there."

"Why not?" she pouted.

"One of the park rangers and I don't get along."

That was the understatement of the decade.

Lacy opened her mouth to argue, but thankfully, Reed tapped on his champagne glass—the universal signal for speeches. He did this at *every* party. I didn't know why, but I was starting to think he just liked the sound of his own voice.

At least this time, it saved me from talking further with his sister.

I listened to him drone on about how it had been such a good year for him and how he'd made so many great memories. I snapped a few photos of everyone looking at him like he was the sun itself.

Even though I was starting to hate him, I at least knew what moments to capture.

"Now," Reed said, "I'd like to invite my lovely girl-friend, Stella, to join me."

My blood turned to ice. I did not want to be in front of these people. Absolutely not. "I'm good right here."

Reed waved his arm.

"Come on!" his brother, Chad, yelled. "Don't tell me

the girl who did drunk karaoke last year now has stage fright!"

I gritted my teeth. The karaoke was what caused the guffaw that his mom still complained about.

"My girlfriend's not shy," Reed said with an easygoing smile. "Come on, dear. Get out here."

"We're wasting time," Patricia groaned before she turned to me. "Don't be difficult about this."

He wouldn't let this go. None of them would. Taking a shaky breath, I made the painful steps over to him.

Gazing at his pretty face, I could see why I liked him two years ago. I'd met him at a client wedding where I'd been running around with my camera in hand, making everyone smile.

"I'll take this," Chad said, reaching for the same camera slung around my neck.

"No, thank you. I'll keep it."

"But it'll ruin the—"

"Stella," Patricia snapped. "Give him the camera."

I glared at them both. "Why can't I keep it?"

"Why do you need to?" she hissed.

My lips pressed together. "This thing is my whole career. I'm not taking it off."

Patricia could have sprained her neck from how hard she rolled her eyes.

I knew the only way to end this argument was to give in. I tamped down the flare of annoyance and handed my camera to Chad. "Fine."

Reed put up his hands in mock innocence. "I promise you'll get it right back."

My wardrobe and my laugh were also a part of who I was, yet they were forced into a box, locked up, and the keys thrown away.

God, I had terrible taste in men.

"I can't believe we've been together for two years," he said, using his speech voice again. He looked around the crowd as if he had forgotten who he was speaking to. "She truly is the light of my life, and I have a surprise for her." He handed off his glass to his brother who had been waiting. He fumbled around in his pocket.

"Wait, what're you doing?" Anxiety rose in me. *No.* He couldn't be—

But he was. Reed grabbed a box out of his pocket and got down on one knee. He opened it, revealing the most basic ring I'd ever seen.

Oh. My. *God.*

Was he really doing this in front of his family? Now?

My breath came out in stutters, panic clawing its way up my throat. My eyes dragged over the people in front of us. Chad was yawning. Patricia glared daggers at me, as she always did whenever she was reminded that I'd stolen her baby boy.

And he wanted me to marry into this?

Winnie would laugh in his face. Nick would tell him off for his shit communication. And I?

I could only take one step back. Then two.

And before I knew it, I was running out the door,

down the hallway, to the elevators, and out onto the street.

Bursting from the building, I realized I didn't have a coat or keys. I was lucky enough to have a phone, so I pulled it out, trying to think of who to call.

Winnie was at work and my parents were at a different party tonight.

That left one person, one who I knew would come with no delay.

My brother.

IN THE LAST SEVEN YEARS, Nick had grown. Gone was the boy who challenged our parents and did what he wanted. Nowadays, he was dependable with a good job and a good apartment.

He apparently still didn't go the speed limit, though, because he arrived in five minutes flat.

"What the fuck happened?" he asked the second he saw me sitting on the side of the road at night in the middle of winter with no coat.

My panic kept me from feeling the cold. The whole time I waited, I was terrified that Reed might come downstairs after me, but he didn't.

He did, however, send a single text.

REED

> You should have said no to my face. I
> hope you find peace, Stella.

It made me sick. Of course he'd look like the better person. Of course he'd tell me to find *peace* when he'd put me on the spot like that. We had never *once* discussed marriage and this was brought up out of nowhere.

The only thing we talked about was how to get me to be better for him.

"Laugh quieter, Stella."

"Wear this color."

"Can you be normal for a bit?"

It was always *me*.

"Reed proposed," I muttered. "It was a surprise."

"And I'm guessing you said no?"

"I didn't say anything. I ran."

"Bold answer."

"And here I am in the ugliest dress I've ever seen, and now I'm single on the weekend before Christmas. Do you know how sad this is?"

"It's pretty sad. Especially the dress. You look like you got the life sucked out of you."

"Thanks for your comfort, Nick." I shook my head. My eyes were watering. Old me would have either gone back up there to give him a piece of my mind or found a nearby bar to wash away my sorrows in.

"Do you want to stay with me?" he asked. "My guest room is open."

"Yes," I breathed out. "Thank you for coming to get me."

"I'll always take care of you," he said. "Especially when you finally break up with your boyfriend."

"Finally? You wanted this to happen?"

He shrugged. "He was weird at the holiday party last year, and you seemed so . . . quiet. It's not like you."

I let out a long sigh and added Nick to the people who saw that Reed was wrong for me before I had truly accepted it. Winnie had been the first to raise the red flag after the guffaw incident. Our grandmother, who we lovingly called Amma, never bothered to remember his name in the first place.

"I should have dumped him sooner."

"Sometimes it takes us all a while to see reason. You'll find someone better."

"Will I? It feels like I've only had duds ever since high school."

Nick rubbed the back of his neck. "There's definitely at least one man who can handle you."

"Is that supposed to be comforting?"

"I'm trying," he said. "But I feel a little weird giving my sister advice on guys."

"I don't need advice," I grumbled. "I think I'm done with them for a bit."

"You are?"

"Yes," I said, standing. "Now, can we get out of here? I'm freezing."

"Get in the car and wait," he instructed. "I'll need your keys."

"I didn't grab them on my way out." I paused. "Wait, why do you need them? You're not about to go up there and yell at Reed, are you?"

"You need a bag, don't you?"

My cheeks heated, the only warmth I could find in this cold weather. "You can go up there. The door shouldn't be locked. But be careful. The Wicked Witch of the West is in there."

"I'll survive."

"Don't get arrested," I said with a sigh. "That's my only request."

He nodded and opened the door to his car for me.

I wasted no time in climbing into the warm embrace of his vehicle. He disappeared quickly and I was left staring into the cold night. Ten minutes later, he had a bag of my stuff.

"Thank you," I said once he'd thrown it in the back seat.

"I had no clue what was all yours. I just dumped colorful stuff in here. I figured it's more your taste than . . ." He gestured to my dress. "Reed said he would gather the rest."

"Is that all he said?"

"That's all *he* said."

"And what did *you* say?"

"I told him a little communication would work in his next relationship. And not putting people on the spot."

My jaw dropped. "You didn't."

"I did. No one messes with my sister."

A warm feeling separate from the heated car wormed its way into my chest. In all the misery that had been that relationship, at least I still had people in my corner.

As we pulled away from the curb, a thought hit me.

"Alden isn't coming over, right?"

Alden and I hadn't talked since he turned me down. Even his name felt foreign in my mouth. He'd treated me like I was a dirty sock after he'd been inside of me, and I refused to forgive something like that. I knew some guys loved to take women's virginity, but I didn't think he was one of them.

Right after it happened, Nick told me it was for the best and that I deserved better. I *did* deserve better, but I'd always wondered what went wrong.

Nick shook his head. "No, he's busy with the park planning for this snowstorm coming in."

I rolled my eyes. "Yeah, a snowstorm. Like Nashville ever gets any of those."

Still, it was cold. Now that the adrenaline was fading, I was realizing how cold I'd actually gotten.

A shiver hit me. I turned to my bag in the back. I was looking for a jacket but came up empty.

"Um, Nick? Did you forget to grab me a jacket?"

"Was there one in your drawers?"

"No. Why would I put a jacket in a drawer?"

"I don't know. I only had a few minutes before I lost it listening to that asshole's mom complain about you."

"I fucking hate her."

"You won't freeze. I have an extra jacket at my place you can borrow."

He turned up the heat as I crossed my arms. "Reed'll probably leave for the Keys with his family tonight, and I'll get my car and other stuff tomorrow. Maybe the next day to be sure he's gone."

"I'll go with you," he said. "If this snowstorm doesn't get us all stuck for a week straight."

I shook my head. "Don't tell me you believe in this stupid thing."

"Amma says this is gonna be a big one."

"Amma wants the snow of her youth," I said. "People always make a big deal of weather and it never turns out to be anything."

"She's really thinking it'll be serious this time. She even wanted my help clearing her porch."

That made me pause. "She asked for help?"

It wasn't like Amma to ask for anything, even though she probably should have assistance in her older age.

"Yeah, but I can't. I have work, and then I need to go get your stuff."

"Why didn't you ask me?"

"I was going to, but you called to ask me to come get you."

"I'll go . . . but can you drop me off before work?"

"Of course I can."

"And pick me up?"

"Yep." He glanced over at me with a smile. "How much is it killing you to have to ask for so much?"

"A six out of ten. I'm still feeling too miserable for my pride to stop me."

"You're not having any feelings of rage or anything?"

"No."

The car lapsed into silence and I glanced over to see his lips were pursed. "You know you're not going to be miserable for long, right?"

"No, I don't know that. For one thing, I might stay single forever at this rate."

"We'll see about that."

"Want to place a bet?"

Nick always loved putting money on odds—no matter how much they were out of his favor.

But he shook his head. "No, I've got enough bets going on right now."

"Enough bets? What kind are you in on?"

"I'll tell you *after* the snowstorm."

"I hope you didn't put your money on us getting snow."

"No. I put it on something much more fun."

* * *

I DIDN'T SLEEP well that night. I dreamed of all the things I could have said to Reed and woke up with a miserable feeling of regret that I'd said *nothing*.

When I got up and looked in the mirror, I didn't

recognize myself. Sure, I was in my own clothes, but the frown etched on my lips wasn't my usual, and my silence felt wrong.

Sure, I wasn't Winnie. I wasn't a powerhouse of a woman who created her own company from the ground up. But I was more vocal than *this*.

I'd gone after Alden Canes for crying out loud, and it *worked*. I got my RA to approve a roommate change request so I could room with Winnie when my first one talked shit about me behind my back. I'd opened my own business, worked with some of the worst bridezillas, and *held my own*.

I wasn't a runner until I met Reed. But now I didn't know how to stop.

When I left the room, I planned to brew a cup of coffee and research ways to overcome a breakup. The emptiness I felt couldn't be normal.

However, I didn't get very far because the kitchen was covered with white.

I blinked, unable to comprehend what was happening in front of me. There was flour on *everything* as Nick attempted to stir something in a bowl. He was the only thing more coated than the countertops.

"What the hell are you doing?" I asked.

"I'm trying to make you breakfast to cheer you up, but I don't fucking know how to cook. You got all those genes, apparently."

"What were you trying to make?"

"Cinnamon rolls, but then I realized that's way out of

my skill set. Then I tried pancakes, but that's *also* too hard for me. Want to show me how it's done?"

Usually, that would be no problem. I loved cooking just as much as I loved eating and photography. But this new version of me hated the thought of trying to make anything. I could still hear Reed's condescending voice telling me all the ways what I put into my food would send me to an early grave.

"I haven't cooked in a year."

Nick blinked. "What?"

"Reed didn't like how I did it. He said it was unhealthy."

He frowned. "Who cares if it's—"

I held up a hand. "Can we not? I'm already feeling bad enough about the last two years. I'd rather go to McDonald's and then to Amma's. Is that okay?"

I would *still* hear how bad fast food was for me, but at least I could ignore it by eating it before I could convince myself to go for something else that I wouldn't like.

Silence stretched between us and I begged Nick to listen. I hadn't cried in front of him since those kids in middle school took my pants in the gym and made fun of how I looked. I wasn't about to break that record now.

"Yeah. Of course. I'll get you whatever you want."

"Thanks. I'll go get dressed."

I walked back to the guest room without another word. When I shut the door, the now-familiar feeling of misery grew.

How much had I given up for Reed? How much of myself was *gone* now?

Rummaging through my bag, I saw all the colors I used to wear, but I felt *nothing* about them. I hadn't for a while. I threw on the first thing I saw and then went to the bathroom to freshen up. Once I was done, Nick was waiting by the door.

"I could kick his ass, you know," he said as I walked out of the room.

"Whose?"

"Reed's. Who else would I be mad at?"

"You have a list of people you don't like."

"Reed is at the top."

"Maybe I'll feel better after food." Doubtful, but worth the shot.

"What about a huge sweet tea too?"

"That might help." I gave him a half smile, which made him perk up.

I was glad he didn't know it was all I could manage.

*　*　*

THE SECOND we pulled into Amma's long, winding driveway, the plume of smoke coming from her chimney was visible.

"Good," I said. "She's got her stove going. It's so fucking cold."

The black puffer jacket Nick had given me the night before was warm, but I only had a sweater underneath it.

If I had my usual closet, I would have layered more. The next-to-zero temperature was the kind of cold Tennessee wasn't used to. We had mild winters with random cold snaps, but it still only got below freezing at night more often than not. Now, it was twelve degrees.

"Before you go in—" Nick reached into the back and pulled out a black duffel. "—I got you this while you were showering."

"A bag? Why?"

"In case it really does snow and you get trapped here."

I rolled my eyes. "I won't—"

"Stella, do it for my sake. It *could* snow, and out here in the country, it might be worse."

His voice was firm, which was unusual for him. While I knew there was no way it would happen like the weather people predicted, the worry in his eyes was obvious.

"Fine." I took the bag from his outstretched hand. "But I'm telling you. We aren't getting that much snow."

"We could make a bet?" he asked.

"I thought you already had one."

"This one is different. It won't involve money."

"Then what are the stakes?"

"Pride."

I didn't have much of that right now, but Nick's worried glances on the way over told me I needed to pretend that I was okay.

"I'll take those odds. If I win, I'll never let you live it down that you were wrong."

"More like I'll never let *you* live it down."

I got out of his warm car into the bitter elements. "Bye!" I called as I shut the door.

The wind blew right through my coat as I ran into Amma's house. Her wooden porch creaked under my feet in a familiar way as I got to the old screen door.

Nick and I spent a lot of time here as kids in the summers when Mom and Dad didn't have childcare. Amma was Mom's mom, and had had a heavy hand in raising us all.

We both had good memories here. Amma always ensured we had fun, whether chasing the neighbor's chickens or jumping into the lake half a mile from her house.

Walking into her small log farmhouse felt like a warm hug I desperately needed. It was a simple abode with a meager living room adorned with an ancient wood-burning stove, keeping the house warm in the cooler months. Behind it was the kitchen, and two bedrooms sat on the left side.

Most of the curtains on the windows were closed, giving it a cozy, darkened feel. The air smelled like the burning wood in the stove, coupled with the warm scent of cinnamon.

"Amma!" I called when I got inside. "I'm here to help you clean off your porch!"

"I'm back in the kitchen," she replied. I shrugged off my coat and went in search of her.

I nearly had a heart attack when I found her

balancing on a ladder, looking at something above the cabinets.

"Oh my God," I hissed. "What are you doing up there?"

"Dusting," she said. "It gets so bad up here over time."

"Dusting? Before a snowstorm?"

"Well, I cleaned the insides of the windows and figured, why not do up here? I don't have the time to clean in the spring. I'm too busy in the garden."

"I'll finish it," I said. "Just get down."

"You worry too much, Stella. I'm fine."

"You asked for help with clearing the porch," I said. "So you know you can't do it all."

"Maybe I invited someone because I wanted the company." She turned to me with a raised eyebrow. "Ever think of that?"

"Is this your way of deflecting?"

"I'll never admit my secrets." She finished dusting as I hovered underneath her in case she fell. "There! All done. Now you don't have to worry."

She hopped down as if it were nothing.

If I reached her age, I hoped I had her nimble nature. Reed had met her once and gave me a long lecture on all the lifestyle changes I would need to make in order to turn out like she did. I hadn't told anyone until Winnie caught me looking up yoga—something I'd never once had an interest in.

The thought of my now ex made my eyes hit the

floor. It wasn't that I missed him. It was that I regretted wasting so much time on him.

"Why do you look so sad?" Amma asked. "That's no way for my favorite granddaughter to look."

"I'm your *only* granddaughter. And it's nothing."

"Come on." She grabbed my hand. "Tell me."

With the warmth of her hand in mine, it gave me enough bravery to take a breath before answering. "Reed and I broke up."

"Reed?" she asked. For a second, she said nothing. Her lips only twisted as she considered the name.

I sighed. "My boyfriend."

"Oh. The skinny one, right? The one at the last Christmas party?"

"Yes."

"I didn't like him too much."

"I didn't either in the end, but it's still two years of my life wasted."

"It was that long?"

"Yes. Everyone knew he wasn't right, but"—I gave a pitiful shrug—"he was my first long relationship."

"We all have our failures in love. I've told you stories of my first husband."

"The one who joined the circus?"

"No, that was the second." She shook her head and then smiled. "See? Even I met a few duds. What was the final straw?"

"He proposed."

"What? Had you even discussed marriage?"

"Nope. Not at all. I was about to dump him, actually. He bought the ring without even consulting me."

Amma shook her head. "Every woman should pick her own ring, or at least have a say. The *proposal* is the surprise."

"Well, it was certainly surprising. Like a horror movie one."

"I'm sorry, Stella. But not entirely sorry. Rather, I'm hopeful for this new phase of your life."

"My single era?"

"If that's what you choose to be. Knowing you, I bet you'll find someone fast."

"Have you *met* me?"

"I have. You're an amazing young woman. When did you start believing otherwise?"

"It started when his mom made fun of my laugh."

Amma's jaw dropped. "How dare she. You have a beautiful laugh."

"Thanks," I said despite my doubt. "It's nice to be with family for a while."

She gave me a warm smile. "As much as I'd love to shower you with more compliments, we do have things to do to prepare for the storm."

"Yeah. Big storm."

"Oh, it will be. I can feel it in my bones."

I didn't have the heart to tell her it would pass over us like most other winter storms. See, Tennessee didn't do this. Sure, we had some snow some years, but it *always* missed or ended up being less than the weather person forecasted.

"Let's get started then," I said. "What do you want moved?"

"The rocking chairs should go in the shed. I don't want any snow on them."

I nodded and put my coat back on before heading outside.

Amma's rocking chairs were solid wood, and moving them proved problematic since the shed was downhill. I couldn't pick them up, so I awkwardly pulled them along. The ill-fitting coat was a hindrance and I wished it wasn't freezing so I could rip it off.

It took me far longer than I wanted to get the two chairs down to the shed and even longer to find space for them. I wound up having to shuffle boxes to make it work.

I was grumbling about how much junk Amma had as I made my way up the hill to her house and to the front door.

But when I reached the top of the hill, I saw a different car had pulled in next to Amma's.

And it was an old, red truck.

The exact one I lost my virginity in.

TWO

ALDEN

"THERE YOU ARE!" Amma said, a wide smile on her face as I walked into her warm house. "Thank goodness. You made it just in time."

The second she saw me, she pulled me into a tight hug. It had been a while since I made it over here, but I usually tried to come to find something to help her with. Amma would rather injure herself than let someone else take care of her cabin for her, but I was also persistent.

"Glad I could make it," I said. "I just got done salting all the paths at the park."

"Will it be open for this?"

"We're always open, and people love to hike in ice." I shrugged. "I have my other ranger, Ryan, staying with me for extra help."

She patted my shoulder. "Good. Then we shouldn't waste time."

"We have about an hour before it starts."

"I need . . . help with something." The words sounded like they pained her.

I paused. "You need *help?*"

She held up a hand. "Don't make this a big deal. I don't need it because I'm sick. I need it because there's too much to do."

I did a once-over on her. Amma wouldn't admit it if she'd hurt herself, but she was standing straight and moved as easily as she always did. "Okay, I'll stay as long as you need."

She smiled. "Perfect. Now, let me show you the windows. I expect to lose power, and the curtains won't hold enough heat in. I need them weatherproofed."

"I just did the same thing on my house. Show me what you have. I'll get it done."

She opened the curtains to reveal the old, weathered windows. They were more than likely original on the house. "You're as responsible as ever, Alden. I can't believe you're still single."

I huffed out a laugh. I could believe it. It was hard to find a girlfriend when I couldn't focus on them. I tried, but they always figured out that there was one woman I had eyes for.

And she was the one I couldn't have.

I couldn't afford to go down the rabbit hole that was Stella Summers—especially not in front of Amma, who noticed everything. She had tried to get us to reconcile over the years, but I refused to talk about what happened.

"Do you have weatherproofing tape?" I asked. "I can go get some if you don't."

Amma put her hands on her hips. "What kind of woman do you take me for? Of course I already have it. It's all in the bag in the living room."

"Good. If I do it right, you'll still be able to see out of the windows."

"That would be nice. I'd love to see the hills covered in snow and ice."

Moments later, I found what I needed and worked from the bedrooms inward. It was simple work, making me wonder why she asked me to do it at all.

However, all thoughts fell away when I saw a figure outside. At first, I thought it was one of Amma's neighbors coming to check on her, but then I realized it was far worse.

It was the very woman I wasn't supposed to think about.

Stella was staring at my truck, undoubtedly wondering what the fuck I was doing here. It took her only seconds to turn on her heel and walk inside.

Shit.

I planned to duck into the bedroom and leave Amma to her questions, but then my eyes caught on her jacket. It was black—a color Stella wouldn't be caught dead in, but it was a North Face jacket with a busted zipper.

My feet moved of their own accord and I walked out the front door.

We came face-to-face in the cold of the porch. Her chestnut brown hair was streaked with gold and her oval face and upturned nose still did unfair things to my heart.

But her forest-green eyes were narrowed, which meant she was pissed.

"Why do you have my jacket?" The words blew out of me.

"I have a better question—what the fuck are you doing here?"

Stella's cheeks were tinted with pink, either from the cold or seeing me. She had dark circles under her eyes that weren't usually there. Coupled with the black jacket, she'd never looked less like herself.

"I—what happened to you?" I asked.

"Nope. Not going there."

Her eyes fell to the frozen ground. Mine widened. Since when didn't she look me in the eye when she was snapping at me?

"Aren't you usually . . . angrier?"

"Do you *want* me to be?"

"Yes."

She rolled her eyes. "You're annoying. How about you answer the damn question?"

That was a little better.

"I'm helping Amma weatherproof the windows."

"No, you're not."

I looked down at the supplies in my hand. "I definitely am."

"I can't deal with this today," she muttered and pushed past me to go inside.

Her vanilla scent filled my nose, the same even after all of these years. My eyes closed, and all I could do was remember the night in my truck when I made the biggest mistake of my life.

I had to take a moment before I followed her.

My jacket hit me in the face the second I walked in the door. "Oh, and you can have that back."

Stella was gone by the time I regained my bearings.

I couldn't resist the smile that made its way onto my face. *That* was the Stella I knew. I'd take her throwing things at me rather than her shying away like she had in middle school when those fucking kids bullied her.

"Stella," Amma said as she walked into the living room, "I know you had a rough night yesterday, but let's be civil."

"I think I'm in the anger stage of grief," Stella replied as she followed Amma. "Spurred on by his presence."

"Who died?" I asked.

"My patience."

"As much as I love watching verbal sparring matches," Amma interrupted, "we have work to do. Stella, I called him here."

"You did?"

"Yes. Him and *Nick*, but he's too busy with work to stay. I can't help that he sent you in his place."

In some way, this was my fault. I didn't tell Nick about my plans since Amma had called me over at the last minute. Half the time, I showed up whenever I hadn't seen her in a while anyway. I doubted he would have sent Stella if he'd known.

"But—" Stella was interrupted by Amma.

"I know you'd love to get all your frustrations out on my other helper, but I can't have that. I want my house to be ready for this weather."

"Amma, this storm isn't a big deal."

"It'll be a very big deal," I interjected. The glare I received in response would have made a lesser man fear for his life. "But we don't have to argue about weather patterns. I'll finish what I started and go."

"I can offer something better," Stella said. "You leave now and I'll weatherproof the windows."

Amma shook her head. "We're on borrowed time here. And I need you for other things."

"What do you need me for?"

"You're the skilled cook in this family. Come and help me meal prep for this."

"*No.*" Stella shook her head firmly. "Amma, I can't. I haven't cooked in a year."

Amma's wide eyes matched mine. Since when did Stella *not* cook? She was always whipping up something in the kitchen—she'd done it even when she was a kid. Oftentimes, when Dad forgot to feed me, I'd go find her. She'd been far too young to work a stove, yet she still made something delicious.

What the hell had happened to her?

My eyes drifted to hers, and she spared me a second of a glance. Her cheeks darkened and she looked at Amma.

"All the more reason to pick it back up," Amma replied once she'd recovered. "Come on. It'll be fun!"

Stella's lips pressed together and I wondered if she'd say no to one of her favorite pastimes. "Fine," she said lowly. "But I can't promise this is going to go well."

"Find me when you're done," Amma said to me as she followed Stella. "I need help with a few more things."

I sighed and put the jacket down on the couch. My body was still buzzing with Stella's proximity and the desire to figure out who the hell had made her like *this*.

But I shook it off, determined to get whatever Amma needed done with so I could leave.

The weatherproofing didn't take me long, but then I was sent to move the couch and ensure enough wood was brought inside so she could keep the house warm. I thought I would be done after that.

The sky was darkening, promising dangerous snow and ice. We were running out of time.

But I wouldn't leave Amma with this.

"Last thing, I promise," she said when I bothered her again. Stella was busy glaring at a recipe like it personally offended her.

"Sure, what is it?"

"Complete this list." She handed me a sheet of paper filled to the *brim* with menial tasks.

"The whole list? Amma, are you sure you're okay?"

Stella finally turned. It seemed she was as worried as I was.

"Oh, I'm fine. Just busy." She smiled and turned back to Stella, who opened her mouth to say something. "And don't you start either, Stella. I'm *fine*."

"Are you?"

"Are *you*?" Amma fired back.

Stella pursed her lips and returned to her cooking. My brows pinched as I watched her. Amma looked just as worried.

Letting out a sigh, I got to work, rushing to complete the list so I could get back to my house. I kept thinking about Stella as I turned over her odd behavior in my mind. I wished my tasks were closer to the kitchen so I could have overheard what they were talking about.

Sometime later, Amma found me working on unclogging the drain in the bathroom.

"Alden," she said, "be a dear and keep an ear on Stella for me. She's cooking right now and I need to go check on something with my neighbor, Hank."

I jerked up from under the sink. She was *leaving*? "Wait—"

"I have to go now if I want to be back before it starts. See you in a few minutes!"

She left so fast that I couldn't get another word out. That woman could *move* when she wanted to.

Being alone with Stella wasn't the best idea, but nothing would happen if I avoided her.

And I highly doubted she would talk to me.

I got back to work, trying not to think about the woman in the other room or the weather rapidly worsening.

Time ticked by, only disturbed by the sounds of me doing errands around the house and Stella banging kitchen pots in the background. It took me far too long to finish the list. By the time I was done, I was in a rush to tell Amma that I had to go.

I'd spent so long working that I assumed she'd already come back and I just didn't hear her. I figured she would be in the kitchen to help Stella with cooking, so I took a chance and poked my head in.

"Amma, I'm going to head out when—"

"Not now," Stella interrupted. "I'm trying to figure out how to explain to Amma that I burned her bread pudding."

I could only stare at her. Stella burned something? Was that even possible? I opened my mouth to ask how when I realized Amma wasn't in the kitchen.

"Is Amma not in here?"

"Nope. She abandoned me to my own cooking, which obviously went poorly."

"Where is she?"

"No idea, Alden. What do you need?"

"I need to tell her I finished the list."

She finally turned to me. "You finished the list? Good. That means you can go."

"I want to check with her first."

"Alden," she snapped, "whatever Amma needs, I'll take care of. Now, will you please go back to whatever park ranger thing you have to do and leave?"

"Fine," I said after a long pause. "I'll go. Just stay safe. She might not be here."

"She's obviously in her room or doing something outside. It's fine."

"There's a snowstorm coming."

"My God, Alden." She turned to me, green eyes full of fire. "Just go. I'm perfectly capable of handling things here, even if there is a massive snowstorm. I'll find Amma and make sure she's okay. The only thing I can't do is deal with you being here anymore."

"Stella."

"Alden." She stepped into my space. "Go."

This was bad. We hadn't been this close in years. The last thing I needed was for her to be so close, especially when I'd never put my feelings for her in a box like I should have.

"If Amma isn't back, call someone."

"I will. I'm not stupid."

But maybe *I* was.

Because I was thinking about staying, even though she was one wrong move away from pushing me out the door herself.

I let out a sigh, turning on my heel to leave.

The second I walked outside, I felt the ice under my feet.

Fuck, it had already started, which meant getting out

of here was going to be a nightmare. I turned once more to the house, tempted to go back inside.

Amma is there, I said to myself. *Stella doesn't want you to stay.*

It was a version of the mantra I told myself each time I stayed away from her. She didn't want me around, which was exactly what she should feel. It made it easier for me to stay the fuck away.

The truck door was stuck shut, and it took me far too long to get it open. Then the truck slid as I was coming out of the driveway. I cursed but managed to keep it on track.

There had to have already been half an inch of ice on the ground, which was way ahead of schedule. I'd studied the forecasts, and there wasn't supposed to be this much this fast.

This was bad. So bad.

Amma is there. Stella is fine.

But as I slowly pulled onto the road, I wondered if I was wrong. If Amma weren't there, then she would be stuck in this alone.

All the warnings I'd heard played back in my head. This area was going to lose power. People could die if they didn't have a backup generator or some sort of fire-place to keep warm.

Amma had a stove, but that was it. She would know how to use it, but would Stella?

The idea of her being alone distracted me just enough from the road to slide off of it. I came to a rough stop, knowing that I could probably get the truck out of the ditch if I worked hard enough. I'd put cat litter in the back seat for this very reason. Still, I would lose valuable time.

Besides, getting *myself* out of it was the last thing on my mind.

THREE

STELLA

I DISPOSED of the charred remains of Amma's bread pudding and hoped she didn't look too closely at the trash. Now that Alden was gone, I was no longer half focused on listening for the noises he was making around the house and I could think straight.

If Amma asked, I was going to blame the burnt food on him.

In reality, I was overwhelmed. Amma helped me make soup, but I got distracted putting it away and forgot to set a timer for the pudding. Cooking used to be second nature to me, but now I felt like it was all new.

And I hated that I felt that way.

I was free to feel the sinking misery again. Alden was a good distraction from it, but the anger was simply a front. I didn't want him to see how low I'd gotten.

"Hey, Amma," I called. "Um, the bread pudding isn't

done, but the soup is. Do you need anything else? I should probably call Nick to get out of here soon."

Only silence answered me.

I paused. I had been *so* sure she had come back. Had I been wrong?

"Amma?" I called again.

The only answer was the blowing wind, which was *loud*.

A prickle of anxiety crawled up my spine.

Then the phone rang.

Amma had one of those wired wall phones—a vintage thing from the nineties. She said she would never get rid of it as long as it worked because she preferred to live without a cell phone.

I didn't know whether or not to answer it. The idea of answering a call at all didn't sound fun, but one without any caller ID sounded worse.

When the answering machine clicked on, I heard Amma's voice.

"Hi, kids," she said. "The weather is getting really bad out there. Don't worry about me. I'm fine, but you might wanna stay where you are. This is a real kicker of a snowstorm. Stay safe, you two!"

My heart stopped. She thought Alden was still here, but he wasn't.

I had kicked him out like a fucking fool.

Maybe Amma was kidding. After all, it couldn't have gotten *that* bad that quickly. I checked the time, eyes bugging out when I saw I'd been cooking for *hours*.

Breath stuttering, I ran out the door, begging the sky to hold off for long enough for me to call Nick and get out of here.

The brutal wind hit me first, and I regretted telling Alden to take his coat back. As I emerged from the porch's protection, my feet slid out from under me, and my back thudded painfully on the gravel below.

Ice crystals hit my face. The strong wind was blowing against the house, bringing pure ice down on the earth.

"No," I groaned. "It's ice."

Ice was less visible. Ice was more dangerous. And it was *everywhere*. I slowly sat up, seeing that Alden's truck was indeed gone.

Oh my God. Could I even survive in this? Did I know how to stoke a fire? Break logs to use in the stove?

Panic made my throat close. I'd managed to keep my cool throughout everything, but *this* was way worse than I could have imagined.

I slowly stood on shaky legs, eyes on the scenery. Ice didn't immediately turn everything white. It instead coated everything in a clear, dangerous concoction. While our area didn't get much snow, we sometimes got ice, but it quickly melted because of the warmer weather.

But we were in a cold front, one destined to last for a long time.

I was hyperventilating. I'd stayed too long. I was too confident.

And then a pair of hands clamped down on my shoulders.

I let out a bloodcurdling scream, my mind going a mile a minute.

Who the fuck was out in this weather? Why were they grabbing me?

And wasn't this ice bad enough? Did I *have* to get murdered too?

I tried to fight back, but it led to me falling onto my knees.

The hands tightened.

"Stella, it's me. It's Alden."

My eyes finally met his. Both of our breaths were quick.

I didn't usually feel relief when Alden was in front of me, but these were not normal circumstances. As much as I hated him, I hated the idea of being alone in this mess of a situation more.

"Wha—why are you out of breath?" I managed to gasp. "Where's your truck?"

"I ran here."

"You *what?*"

"I didn't know for sure if you were alone or not. And I'm not leaving you in this."

I didn't understand. He'd left me before. He should *easily* be able to do it again.

But even with our past, relief made my eyes water. The panic ebbed, replaced with the feeling of gratitude that Alden may have broken my heart, but he didn't leave me in this ice storm.

"Why didn't you drive back?" I asked, eyes on the empty driveway.

"The truck went off the road about half a mile out."

"So, you're stuck here?"

"I could have—" He paused. "Would it make you feel better if I said yes?"

"You chose to be here? In *this*?"

He nodded.

My jaw dropped. It was then I realized that I was still in his grip and that I had the stupid urge to lean into it to shield myself from the cold.

I wrenched myself away, reminding myself just what Alden had done to me.

"This is a disaster. Can we get to your truck? Can we get out?"

His eyes looked back at the road. "It's getting worse fast. We could try but . . . the rule number one about driving in ice is that you *don't*. I'm not risking your life right now."

"You're a park ranger."

"And I know when it's dangerous."

"I think I'd rather die than be stuck here."

"Not an option."

His voice was forceful and I shook my head. "No, I—"

"Stop arguing." He held out the jacket. "Put this on."

"The jacket? You ran with it?"

"Yes."

None of this made sense. "I don't—"

"Stella," he snapped. His hand cupped my cheek and it felt hot against my skin. "You're freezing."

"S-so?"

"Put the jacket on."

I leaned away. "No."

"Then get inside before you freeze."

My stomach flipped at the sound of him telling me what to do, and the memories of seven years ago burned despite the cold. I was holding onto my last shred of dignity like a vise, and if I had done what I was told, it might as well have been thrown out the window.

And it was *him*. I may have lost everything, but Alden Canes wouldn't tell me what to do.

"No. I'm going to sit here and think about ways not to be stuck with you."

"Stella, it's zero fucking degrees outside. How about you quit being stubborn and let me help you?"

"Never."

"Jesus Christ," he muttered. I thought he would give up, but I should have known better.

Alden got to his feet, pulling me with him. I tried to resist, but then he picked me up and slung me over his shoulder like I was a sack of potatoes.

"What the—Alden, put me down!"

"You have five feet to shut the fuck up and let me do something for you."

The walk was short-lived, just as he said, and he dropped me on the couch. I would have felt the blessed warmth of Amma's house if I wasn't already seething.

"Don't touch me again."

"I don't plan to—unless your stubbornness gets in the way of your judgment. I'm not letting you freeze to death because of your pride."

Now that I was inside, I knew he was right. The cold had settled into my fingers, and they still felt like pure ice despite the warmth around me. My teeth chattered and things would have been worse if he hadn't stepped in.

There had only been one time I'd seen the weather turn this bad. We'd all bundled up and hunkered down until it melted, but in true Tennessee fashion, it warmed up and entirely melted only two days later. This time, the forecast was calling for the temperature to stay below freezing for the foreseeable future.

Reality hit me hard. I should have listened to the weather. I should have never come here and downplayed it. And now I was locked in Amma's tiny house with Alden *fucking* Canes.

My body was already shaking, but now my emotions made it even worse. All the fight drained out of me. I was an idiot and now I suffered the consequences. I wouldn't survive this week, not with the cold hostility added to the room surrounding us.

I heard the door to the wood-burning stove open, making me look up.

Alden wasn't glaring at me anymore. Instead, he was adding logs to the fire. The heat from the opened door curled around the room, chipping away at the ice that had formed around me.

"I'm sorry," I said. "I shouldn't have acted like a brat out there."

He paused and turned to me. "Excuse me?"

Oh God. I'd never live this down. "I said I'm sorry. Do you have to make this a thing?"

"You don't apologize, Stella. Usually you take whatever you're wrong about to the grave."

Old me would have. New me couldn't even look him in the eyes. "Guess I'm not the girl you knew."

"Who the hell did"—he gestured to me—"this."

"Why does it matter?"

"Because this isn't you."

"And how do you know who I am?"

He raised an eyebrow. "I've known you your whole life."

"Not for the last seven years you haven't."

His lips pursed, and he turned back to the fire. Our conversation froze over like the ground outside.

"Besides," I said, "this is going to be easier if I *don't* be the person you know."

"Not for me, it won't." His voice was low.

"What does that mean?"

"It means it's easier if you're *you*. I don't like seeing you fold into yourself like this."

"The other option is me being angry."

"Then be as mad as you want, Stella. In fact, I welcome it."

"No man in his right mind would want to be stuck with *me* when I'm mad."

He slowly turned. "I never said I was in my right mind."

My brain couldn't comprehend that he'd come back, much less what he was saying. Was I still in the snow? Was I dying and dreaming all of this up?

That would be the only way this would make any sense.

Alden didn't like me. It took me a long time to see it, but he only tolerated me because of his relationship with Nick.

Sure, he said he found me physically attractive once, but if that had been true, he obviously regretted it.

I used to think it was his loss. But these days, it felt more like mine than anything else.

Why did I ever think sleeping with him was a good idea? I should have let it be. We would have stayed friends at the very least, and I would have one less man making me feel like I wasn't enough.

Winnie would kick my ass if she knew how much I was spiraling about who I was. She was fearless, always staying true to who she was even when people looked down on her. I wished I could be that way, but after spending two years being told I was too much, it had started to sink in.

And now I was stuck with the man who was my first rejection.

My first *heartbreak*.

This was *not* going to be a fun week.

FOUR

ALDEN

When I finished stoking the fire, I expected to see Stella glaring at me. Instead, she was folded on the couch as if trying to be as small as possible.

I had to do a double take, just like when she'd apologized. Had I been sent back in time to when she was in middle school?

"Stella?" I asked.

Her eyes flickered to me. "What?"

"Are you okay?"

"Don't pretend to care."

My throat went dry. I *did* care. Far more than I should.

What I *should* do was let her have her privacy. Helping her might make her do anything else but hate me, and that was the last thing I needed.

Nick was going to have to kill me, because when

Stella Summers was like *this*, I wasn't going to sit on my ass and do nothing.

"Amma mentioned you were in a bad mood. What happened?"

"I don't want to talk about it."

"Okay." I didn't blame her for her distrust, but I couldn't keep my mouth shut as I saw her curl in on herself further. "Don't do that."

"Do what?"

"Try to make yourself smaller because I'm here. Take up space. Be yourself."

"You don't like it when I'm myself."

"Now I know I never said that."

Her eyes shot to me, but I held firm. I remembered the exact words of my text. I'd replayed them for years.

"Fine. Then other people have."

"Then they're fucking idiots. All of them."

"You think so?"

"Absolutely."

Slowly, she smiled, and it felt like winning the Super Bowl.

"Fine. Maybe they were. But for the record, I think *you're* also an idiot."

"Why?"

"Because you chose to be stuck with me."

I'd been stuck with her my entire life, even when I tried not to be. But she followed me, even when she wanted nothing to do with my life.

"We can say I couldn't get the truck out if it makes you feel any better."

"So we lie?"

"I'm good at lying."

"Good at lying? Since when—"

The wind interrupted her words as it hit the house with a vengeance. The wood creaked and my eyes moved to the windows. Amma took care of her house, but it was old, and any of the glass could shatter if the wind hit it right.

As the seconds turned into minutes listening to the powerful winds, I prayed Amma's ancient cottage held up.

Then an arm hit mine. "This feels like the beginning of a horror movie."

Stella had gotten up and shuffled closer to me. I had to do a double take again to be sure I was seeing things right. It had been years since she was this close. Her hair was almost touching the sleeve of my flannel and her arm was a mere inch from mine.

I shook off the shock of it. She wasn't close by because she wanted to be. She was here because she was scared.

"Heavy winds were predicted," I said lowly. "Don't worry."

Stella came an inch closer. Now, her whole arm was pressed into my side, and I had to grit my teeth and avert my eyes. "Then why are you glaring at the walls like they're offending you?"

"I'm listening to be sure the windows don't break. Amma has very old ones." *And trying not to think too much about how close you are.*

"What if a tree falls?"

"It's a possibility."

Her eyes went to the wall. Before I could stop myself, my hand went to her back. Stella's breaths came out in stutters and she didn't pull away.

I shouldn't be touching her like this, and I definitely shouldn't feel any sort of pleasure that she let me do it, but a white-hot heat erupted from where my hand touched her. It made it impossible to pull away.

We stayed still as the wind pounded on the house.

When it died down, only silence remained.

"Everything is so quiet," she said in a hushed tone.

The second she did, my phone went off.

"Okay, never mind."

I took out my phone and nearly cursed. Nick was calling, and it reminded me that I'd let Stella get far too close.

"I need to take this," I said, stepping away from her. Her hand reached out, and I dodged it, heart in my throat. "I'll be in the kitchen. Stay here."

I walked away before I could convince myself to stay.

Nick needed to know who I was stuck with. I'd skated around Stella for years, never letting myself get too close, but there was no way I could do that while stuck in the same house as she was. He wasn't going to be happy, but it wasn't in my plan to let anything happen.

I hoped he believed me.

"Alden, did you see the snow on the ground? I've never seen anything come down so fast!" He sounded childlike, and I didn't blame him. He loved the snow.

"I'm unfortunately not seeing snow. Only ice."

"Oh, that's not as fun. Where are you?"

I closed my eyes, readying myself for his anger. I felt like I was twenty-two again, about to tell him I had slept with Stella. That had been one of the worst things I'd ever said to him, and while I promised myself I would never put myself in a position to have him that mad at me again, it seemed fate had other plans.

"Amma's house."

Nick went silent. "You're at Amma's house? Funny. I just sent Stella there."

"Yep. She's here too."

"Amma must have her hands full."

"She would if she were here. But she got stuck at the neighbor's house." There was only silence on the line. I couldn't wait for his response, so I kept talking. "Anyway, I don't know if I can get out of here, and this cold front is supposed to last for three days at the very least."

"So it's *just* you and Stella?"

I winced. My dedication to staying away from Stella had ensured that Nick and I could remain friends, but now everything was in danger.

"Yes."

I waited for him to snap at me to stay the hell

away from her. Sure, he'd matured a lot over time, but this was still his little sister who he'd do anything for.

"Do you guys have food and water?" he asked instead. I hadn't even thought of it yet. I'd been too focused on Stella to check.

"Y-yeah." I checked the fridge. "Amma and Stella cooked a little, and it looks like Amma has a pile of . . ." I went to the counter where boxes from a local bakery were stacked. "What are these, muffins?"

"Blueberry or chocolate chip?"

"Is that what's important right now?"

"Your sanity is important, and if Stella doesn't have chocolate chip muffins, she might kill you. Maybe that'll happen either way."

"You seem . . . calm about this."

"I'm putting up a front," he said, an awkward chuckle escaping him. "I thought this storm would be kind of fun, but now I'm hearing the news say people could die, and I find it far less fun."

"We should be fine here. The stove is burning, so it won't be too bad when we lose power."

"*When* you lose power?"

"It's inevitable out here. If it hadn't been going when I got here, I would have made sure it was."

"You guys will be okay, right? Like the stove will keep you warm and stuff?"

"We'll be fine. I know how to survive in this. I'll keep her safe."

"Good." He let out a breath of air. "Hearing about these kinds of things is way less scary than living them."

"I knew it would be bad the second I saw the radar. It's why I came to help Amma. We just lost track of time."

"Amma does that to people. Take care of her, okay?"

"Who, Amma? She's not here—"

"No, Stella."

Take care of Stella? What? Had he truly forgotten what happened?

"I will," I said. "Like she's my own sister."

I hated calling her that. I certainly didn't feel any sort of *familial* feelings for Stella at all, but I would pretend to if it meant Nick knew how serious I was about staying away from her.

"Er, yeah. Sure. Listen, I've gotta go. I was supposed to pick Stella's stuff up from her ex's apartment, but now I'm stuck in traffic on an ice rink."

"Stella's *ex*?"

"Long story. Hey, if you manage not to piss her off, maybe she'll tell you. Talk to you later, Alden!" And then he hung up.

And I was left confused, waiting for the warning that hadn't come.

Obviously, the years had made Nick trust me again— so much so that he didn't even feel the need to state the obvious.

I wouldn't betray that trust. Not again. Despite my displaced attraction for her, I wouldn't act on any of it. I'd give her the space she needed and stay out of the way.

Easy enough.

FIVE

STELLA

I ALWAYS THOUGHT that I'd be fearless in the face of danger.

But when the wind sounded like it was about to knock down the house, I was a fucking coward. I knew that I would be the first to die in a horror film purely because I didn't want to move. An axe murderer could come for me and I would stay in place like the most boring target alive.

Huddled on the couch, I watched every window while Alden was gone. It felt easier when he'd been here because he knew what he was doing. There was no way I could have made it through this on my own, and that was a humbling thought.

A creak echoed through the house, making me jump up from the couch. "Alden! The house is falling."

I felt him at my back before I saw him. He was warm and firm behind me, a comfort in the face of whatever the hell was happening. I didn't know how he'd even gotten here so fast—he must have run from the kitchen.

The house *did* sound like it was coming apart, but as soon as it started, it was over.

"Are we alive?" I croaked as silence took over again.

"That was outside." He went to look out the window. "A big tree branch fell."

"O-oh, is that all?" I laughed awkwardly. "It sounded bad. Sorry."

"It would have been if it were closer to the house." He gestured for me to walk over, and through the window film, I could see the brown all over the ground. "See how big it is?"

It was from Amma's maple, a massive thing older than the house.

I looked up at him. This close, I could see the streaks of green in his normally brown eyes and the way his five-o'clock shadow darkened his lower face. My heart did a flip. It was honestly unfair that he was this attractive.

"T-the wind did this?"

"It often does. Luckily for us, we can trim it and use it for firewood." He walked to the couch where his jacket sat.

"You're going out there now?"

"Yep. We'll need more soon."

"Won't you be cold?"

He pulled gloves out of his pocket. "I'll be fine. Stay here."

I opened my mouth to beg him not to leave but then closed it. I needed to be less of a coward about this.

Even though reality gripped me like a vise, I would remain strong and not let my fear show again. Nor would I get so close that I could see every detail of his face.

Both were bad for my pride.

It didn't matter that my life had blown up. It mattered that I kept it together while I was trapped with the man who hated me. It mattered that I *appeared* okay, not that I was.

I went and sat on the couch, choosing to doomscroll social media instead of dealing with my problems. All I saw were reminders of them since everyone was talking about the disastrous storm outside.

After twenty minutes of being alone, I got up to be sure Alden hadn't frozen to death. I peered out the window. I couldn't see well, but I could see the blurry outline of an axe in his hand. He was chopping the branches with a full-body swing that *almost* made me want to go outside and see it in person.

He *had* picked me up like I was nothing. Had anyone managed to do that before?

What would he look like in full detail? Would his hair be falling out of place? Would his jaw be ticced?

No. *No.* I was not going to swoon over him, no matter how good his silhouette looked in the window.

If it were anyone else, this could have been a scene

from a romantic movie. Two people stuck in a house. What could happen?

But in this situation, it was only pain. I'd seen this ending before and I didn't like it very much.

I shook off the thoughts, shutting the curtains. I was in a delicate state, newly single, with most of my things in a place I was no longer welcome. I wouldn't even have my camera for a week, and I wasn't used to not having a way to document my life.

The last thing I needed was to drool over Alden and have my brother's best friend break my heart for the second time.

I busied myself with gathering blankets from the closets in case tonight was freezing. The Christmas tree twinkled innocently in the corner, and it hit me that the holiday was in a few days, and no one had any idea of where we'd be. When I was a kid, we dreamed of snow on Christmas. Now it seemed more like a nightmare.

My hands stilled as I realized, for the first time in my entire life, my family wouldn't be together.

Fuck. This was just another thing to add to the mounting reasons that everything was *bad*.

Tears welled in my eyes as I remembered all our traditions that wouldn't be happening. There would be no breakfast casserole, no home-cooked dinner that all of us gathered around the table for, and no movies by the fire.

Christmas was sacred. It was the one warm glow in a

dark and dreary season. I looked forward to it every year, but it didn't seem to be happening this time.

Damn it. Why couldn't I keep cool? Why was I so upset about missing one stupid holiday?

Between the bad proposal, having to temporarily move in with Nick, and this snowstorm, everything felt like it was falling apart.

Blindly reaching for my phone, I knew I needed my best friend.

She would be away from work because of the storm unless she were stubborn enough to stay at the office. Her job as a CEO sometimes came before everything else.

Except for me.

"Holy shit, Stella," Winnie said the second she answered. "I've seen three wrecks on my way home. What is happening?"

"I'm glad you didn't stay at the office. You'd be trapped."

"I love my business, but not *that* much. I left right when the dark clouds of apocalypse gathered."

Speaking of weather, the wind returned with a vengeance, making the house whine. I winced against the noise.

"What the fuck is that?" Winnie asked. "Are you outside right now?"

"No. I'm at Amma's. I'm stuck here."

"In the country? Is it worse there?"

"Very. A tree already fell."

"She better not be out there cutting it."

"She's not here at all. She's trapped at a neighbor's house."

"Are you alone?" Winnie sounded panicked, and I had no doubts that she would come and get me herself.

"No," I said, and she blew out a breath of relief. "Worse. Alden is also stuck here."

"Wait a second, *Alden*? As in Nick's Alden? How the fuck did that happen?"

"Amma wanted more help."

"That's *bad*."

"I can't do this. This stupid storm is going to last past Christmas with my family, and then on top of that, I'm trapped with the first man in a long line of them who freaking hates me."

"He only hates you *romantically*."

"That doesn't help!"

"Sorry," she said. "I know it doesn't. But think about it this way—he knows you. It's not a stranger. Let's try to see the positives."

"Would you be able to see the positives if you were stuck with Nick, of all people?"

"Okay . . . no. I wouldn't."

"And it sounds like a fucking horror movie here. I'm literally losing my mind."

"First of all, take a breath."

"I don't want to."

"You *need* to."

Against my wishes, I sucked in a breath, if only to

prove her wrong. But then I felt a tiny bit better, and I knew she'd been right.

"What now?"

"Have you eaten?"

"Just a McMuffin a few hours ago."

"Yeah, that doesn't cut it. What are your options there?"

"Amma made me meal prep some soup. She has this stack of muffins too. What are those even for?"

"Probably to live off of if the power goes out."

Oh, *God.* "I can't even think about that."

"So, soup?" she asked, getting me back on track.

"Yeah. I have soup. It was the only thing I didn't burn. I'm throwing some in the microwave now."

"All right, see? Things are a little better."

"What do I do for the next few days?"

"Survive."

"Is there really a chance the power will go out?"

"Yes. This is going to be *hard* on our electric grid. The city is talking about rolling blackouts, and people in rural areas are already losing power."

"*Fuck.* What do I even do if we lose power?"

"Amma has a fireplace, right?"

"It's a stove, but yes. And thanks to Alden, we have logs."

"There you go," she said. "Stay calm, and focus on staying warm. This isn't about who you're with. This is about getting out of this in one piece."

"Couldn't it have been with anyone else?"

"Not really. Nick wouldn't know how to handle this, and neither would I. This could be a good thing."

That wasn't what I wanted to hear. "I don't want to depend on him."

"Stella," Winnie said. "Put your pride away."

My mouth zipped shut. If *Winnie* was telling me to put my pride away, then it was serious.

"This isn't going to be fun," she continued, "but this is the hand you've been dealt. I wish you were at home but—"

"I don't have a home. Reed and I broke up."

"Oh. So you're *really* not okay."

"It's for the best. He was an ass."

"He was. You know how I felt about him. The way he talked to you was unacceptable."

"I know, and though it took me way too long to see it, I finally did. But the point is, I'm not okay, and I don't want Alden to see that. At least not more than he already has."

"I know. I would be in the same boat as you, but like I said, this isn't about pride. It's about surviving."

I let out a sigh. I'd already put some of it away when I'd huddled up to him in the eerie sounds of the wind. I didn't even think twice about it—I'd found the nearest person and ran to them. It didn't matter that Alden had broken my heart once, he was there.

But he wasn't going to be there for me any more than he had to be. The second he got a call, he was gone and away from me. I needed to remember what we were now —not what we'd once been.

Now that I was on the phone with someone else, I saw how dumb it was to look to *him* of all people for support. While he'd never said it, I knew he saw me as his best friend's annoying sister. It was why he sent that text after his post-nut high was gone.

"I don't want to do this," I whispered to Winnie. "Being around him is bringing up all of those things that happened seven years ago. And I don't want to rehash the past right now. I can't."

"Then don't," she said. "You know what happened. You don't have to talk to him about it. The only thing you have to do is survive."

I sniffled and nodded. As much as I'd love more insight into his decision, she was right. I didn't need it. Definitely not now when we had nowhere to go. "Okay," I said. "God, I'll miss you. We won't even get to do our Christmas Eve dinner."

"We'll make up for it, I promise. And when we do, you can tell me everything that happened with Reed and I can kick his ass."

I laughed despite my misery. "I can't wait."

"And if Alden hurts you again, I'll kick his ass too."

"I think it's inevitable at this point. Everything hurts right now. I don't feel like myself."

Winnie was silent for a long moment, and I wondered if she was about to give me one of her patented lectures to get me off of my ass and back to my old self. As much as I loved her ferocity, I didn't think it would work this time.

"We'll get you feeling better once this is over, okay?" she said instead, and I couldn't fight the relief I felt.

"Okay."

"And stay safe. That's the most important thing to me. Everything else going on can be fixed later, but not if you freeze in this storm. I need to make a few other calls, so I'll talk to you later, okay?"

I hated that she had to leave, but her job kept her busy, so I said my goodbyes and hung up. Once I was alone again, I felt my misery for all of one minute before I put it away.

This was about surviving. I'd do well to remember that.

SIX

ALDEN

I was covered in ice, but I knew that if I went back inside and Stella huddled up to me again, I'd be in a different kind of trouble.

She was too close. Too close and too tempting. It was easier to freeze outside than to burn in her presence.

I'd chopped way more firewood than I needed when my phone rang, bringing me out of my thoughts. At first, I thought it was Nick again. Maybe he remembered that he needed to tell me to stay away from Stella.

Instead, it was a number that I didn't recognize.

I didn't answer.

But then a text came through.

UNKNOWN NUMBER

Alden Canes. Answer the fucking phone.
It's Winnie.

I had to stare at it for a few seconds. How the fuck did Stella's best friend have my number?

Then my phone rang again and I knew I would be in mortal danger if it really was Winnie and I continued ignoring her. "Hello?"

"Finally." Her tinny voice was laced with irritation. "What is with our generation and not answering the phone?"

"Scam calls."

"Then you yell at them like a normal person. God."

"How do you have my number?"

"I called fucking *Nick*, of all people. If that's not dedication to my best friend, I don't know what is."

I blinked in shock. She called Nick? The man she hated?

The world around me might have frozen over, but I didn't know Hell had too.

"Why did you need my number?"

"Because you're stuck with my best friend, that's why. Nick tried to tell me it would be fine, but I knew I needed to make sure you know a few things if you're going to be stuck with her."

"Hang on, Nick tried to tell you it would be fine?"

She huffed out a breath. "Yes, he did. Something about how you won't hurt her or something. I stopped listening about halfway through, as I usually do. But I'm not calling to talk about him. I'm talking about Stella."

I scrubbed a hand over my face. "What about her?"

"You know I'd murder for her, right? That woman is

the light of my world, and her stupid ex dulled her shine. I am *not* about to let you continue that trend."

"I'm not trying to make her feel worse—"

"Sure, yeah. You don't like her, and you've got your reasons for it. I don't care about those. She's scared. She's newly single, and this will be her first Christmas without her family. Think about that for a second."

I closed my eyes as the words hit me. Winnie was right. This was Stella's favorite holiday, and the timing of this storm hadn't fully come together in my mind. I'd made peace with the fact that the holiday this year was a bust some time ago. I doubted she'd done the same.

A war was happening inside of me. I needed to stay away from her. But I didn't want to. She'd still been one of my best friends until I broke her heart, and she was hurting right now.

Nick wasn't here this time to police me, and as much as I should have been scared of what he would say, I found that I was more worried about Stella.

"I know this is gonna be tough for her."

"So, are *you* going to make it tough? Are you going to act pained to see her, or are you going to put away your stupidity and be her friend again?"

I was silent. I didn't know how to be friends with Stella. I only knew how to want more.

"Oh my God," Winnie said. I could hear the eye roll in her voice. "Is it this hard for you? You used to hang around her all the time, and after you had sex with her, you left. You're no better than the kids who made fun of her for wearing colors."

"Excuse me?" I snapped. "I've never said that was the problem."

"Struck a nerve, did I? I've got news for you, buddy. You made her feel like they did. It doesn't matter what justification you tell yourself—you left. By never talking to her, she got the message loud and clear. Are you going to continue that trend?"

I gritted my teeth, knowing going toe-to-toe with Winnie wasn't in my best interest. I knew Stella didn't like me, but I tried my best to believe that she'd kept her head high and never thought *she* was the problem when it came to our doomed one-night stand.

"No," I said. "I'm not."

"Good. Because if another man makes her feel like she's not enough, I might go to jail. Get over whatever bullshit you're feeling, Alden, and treat Stella like a queen like she deserves."

She hung up without another word. I let out a sigh when she did. Winnie was a terrifying woman, but she managed to say the one thing that would throw my plan out the window.

SEVEN

STELLA

I WAS HALFWAY through my soup when I got a text.

WINNIE

I decided to be proactive and go ahead
and threaten Alden. You should be
good now.

Winnie. No. I thought you said we didn't
have to talk about it.

YOU don't have to talk about it, but
someone needs to tell him what a dick
he is.

I didn't have time to process what she had before the
door swung open and Alden walked in. My eyes flew to
him, only to find him already looking at me.

My frazzled brain struggled to come up with

anything to say. Did I apologize on behalf of Winnie or did I tell him he deserved it?

He opened his mouth and I settled on an answer before he could speak.

"Don't worry about what Winnie said. You don't have to be nice to me. I'm good."

"I wasn't . . . How did you know she called?"

"She told me. And I get it. She's worried, but she has no reason to be. I'm fine."

"You're not fine. Even I can see that."

Okay, then. I guess I wasn't lying my way out of this. "Maybe I'm not fine, but you don't have to force yourself to be nice to me. I don't care what she threatened you with—"

He let out a long sigh. "It wasn't much of a threat. She only told me how I made you feel. That was enough."

"What—you didn't know you hurt me?"

"I know I did," he said. "But I didn't know that it made you question . . . *you*. That was never my goal."

"It's what happened."

He looked away, eyes falling to the ground. "You don't have to forgive me. Or want to talk to me. We don't have to be best friends, but this will be a little easier if we at least talk . . . I think."

"You *think*?"

"No, I know." He shook his head, lips pursed. Was he . . . frustrated with himself?

Our conversations, even as kids, never carried this

weird energy. Alden seemed to be at war with himself over something as simple as this.

"It's fine. Surviving doesn't require talking."

"Do you have experience with that?"

My eyes flew to him. "What the hell does that mean?"

"You look worn out, like you've been in survival mode for too long." At my answering glare, he put up his hands. "Hey, you don't have to answer. I was just pointing out a fact."

"How about we talk about something else," I muttered. I wondered if he could even come up with anything.

"What kind of soup is that?"

My eyes sank to my bowl. I'd forgotten I was even eating.

"Chicken and gnocchi."

"Amma's recipe?"

"Kind of. I added a few things to it."

"How is it?"

"Why do you care?"

"You've always been good at cooking." He shrugged. "It's been a while since I've had anything you made."

When we were kids, I would shove my experiments at both Nick and Alden, eager to have other people taste my cooking. It had been a long time since I'd forced a taste test of my most recent creation into his mouth. It had stopped like all other communication after that fateful night.

And despite everything, I wanted him to try it. I wanted his opinion.

I held out the spoon. "Here. Try some."

Alden didn't waste time grabbing the spoon. I unhelpfully remembered the times when I used to spoon-feed him, which made my body flush.

His lips curved around the utensil, and yet another terrible thought hit me.

That's an indirect kiss.

Goddammit. I'd spent only minutes with him and my childlike thoughts were rushing back to me.

"This is incredible."

I hated that I perked up. "Really? Even the cream of chicken base? I made it myself."

"You can make that?"

"You can make anything if you have the time for it. Or the willpower. I'm a bit rusty, though. It could have used more cream and—"

"Is there more?"

All of the words fizzled out of my brain. I nodded and watched as he got his own bowl. My cheeks heated. There were no questions about what was in it or how many calories it was.

God, I missed that.

I missed *this*—the easy banter we used to have.

"Why haven't you cooked in a while?" he asked as he sat with his own bowl.

"I answered the soup question. I don't have to answer anymore."

"Fine. I get it. But all I know is what I've heard, and if anyone told you to stop cooking, then they're a fucking idiot."

"I'm actually the idiot here. I let someone walk all over me for far too long."

"Who?"

I glanced at him again. His posture was stiff and his grip on the spoon tightened.

"You don't need to pretend to be protective over me. Those years have passed."

"I'm not pretending."

"Why would you—"

"I don't have a right to feel the way I do, not after what I did. I know that, but I don't like the idea of anyone walking all over you, Stella. You deserve better."

It was such a shocking statement that it knocked my defenses loose. I answered before I could stop myself. "His name is Reed. I dated him for two years."

"Reed sounds like the name of a jackass."

"That's . . . I'm sure there are nice Reeds out there."

"Maybe there are. But am I right about this one being a jackass?"

"Not in the obvious ways. But as far as cooking, he hated anything that I made. He had to know only healthy things were going into it. No salt, sugar, or . . . fun."

"I'm pretty sure all of those are good in moderation."

"Reed was *very* worried about his health."

"Was, huh? Did he die?"

"No. But he's dead to me. It's over as of almost twenty-four hours ago."

"Do you . . . want to talk more about it?"

I eyed the way his shoulders were *still* tense. "Next time you ask that, try not to look so pained."

"We don't really know each other, but we're stuck together so . . ." He looked away, face twisted as if he knew exactly how awkward this was.

We don't really know each other, but he'd taken my virginity. Yeah, whatever.

"How about we pretend we're fine and move on, okay? We don't have to talk about it."

"You'll never be able to pretend you're fine and me not pick up on it, Stella."

I blinked. "How did you still catch it? Most people don't see it."

"I'm not most people."

I dared to glance over at him again. With his rough exterior, he looked nothing like the last four men I'd dated. Yet we had ended with the same conclusion that all of my other relationships had.

There was something wrong with me.

"Have to cancel any photography sessions?"

The question nearly made me drop my spoon. "You're asking about my life?"

"Is that a safe topic? Or should we spend the next few days in silence?"

I was tempted to say silence, but even I knew I couldn't survive that.

"None other than the one my stupid boyfriend had me working," I answered. "I lighten my workload around the holidays to spend time with my family, which obviously isn't going to happen now."

"A lot of plans are dashed," he said. "Mine are too."

"Your plans with us, you mean?"

"I do other things with other people, you know."

"Like what? Spending time with a girlfriend or something?"

As far as I knew, Alden didn't do long-term girlfriends. I didn't know how I would have handled it if he did. Sure, he had on-and-off girlfriends in high school, but I was a green-eyed monster even then. Nowadays, I'd love it if I was over that feeling, but even the idea made my spine straighten.

Maybe I'd never be over my first heartbreak.

"Not exactly," he replied. I tried not to let the relief show on my face. "I usually find a place to go hike at on Christmas."

"Why?"

"The quiet is good for me."

I could see him walking alone in nature. I'd never considered hiking in my adult life because it was always associated with Alden. Despite how much he had hurt me, I wondered what it was like to be on those walks with him.

The wind blew again, stopping any conversation. I turned to the window in the dining room. This was one of the few without curtains since Amma liked to look out of it while she ate her breakfast.

Slowly, the world outside had only gotten worse.

While being stuck in this house was a nightmare, the scenery outside was still beautiful. I didn't often get to see the trees and ground covered with glistening ice. Eventually, it would be covered with white snow, but for now, I bet I could get some incredible shots—if only I had my camera.

New note to self: take it *everywhere*.

"What's that look for?"

"I don't have my camera. It feels like I'm missing a limb."

"A camera, huh?" His lips twisted into a smile. "I'll be right back."

He got up and went to the living room where he grabbed an eighties Polaroid. "Amma had me pull this out of her room. There's also more of the film. I have no idea if it works."

"More of the film as in film packs?" I asked.

"Yeah, I think so. They looked newer."

I nearly ran back to the living room to find them. I'd used Amma's Polaroid when I was a kid. I knew the camera would still work so long as the film packs did. I found them on one of her side tables and loaded in a new one before going back to the dining room.

"Smile," I said to Alden before shooting a picture.

He only had time to turn before the camera flashed.

Moments later, it printed a picture of him looking like a deer in headlights.

"You got it to work?"

"And look at this great shot I got. You're a natural." I showed him the picture, and he rolled his eyes.

"You're being sarcastic, aren't you?"

"Very." I smiled at him. "But thank you. At least I'll have something to remember this hellscape by."

"You *want* to remember something bad in photos?"

"Life is full of all of it. So why wouldn't I? Besides, it can't get any worse than this."

He raised his eyebrows, but then the power flickered. I frowned and looked at the ceiling light. "What was that?" I asked.

"I'm guessing you don't know the cardinal rule of survival."

"And what's that?"

"Never say things can't get worse."

Like a curse, the lights flickered once more. And then they completely went out, leaving us in darkness.

EIGHT

"Apparently, over ten thousand people in rural areas don't have power," Melody Summers, Stella's mom, said over FaceTime. "The ice is weighing down the lines, and the wind is making it worse. They've even warned the city that our power could go too. I'm surprised the phones are even still working. The cell phone towers must have emergency backup power."

"And that won't last forever," Stella said. "This is a nightmare. When I talked to Winnie earlier, she mentioned even the city might have rolling blackouts."

"Glad we have a fireplace at our house."

"This isn't how I wanted to spend Christmas." Stella sighed and rubbed her forehead. "I hate this."

"We'll get together after all of this is over," Melody reassured her. "And we'll make it extra special for getting through this storm. Now, do you know how to make a fire?"

"I know how to," I replied, coming into frame. I hadn't made myself known simply because I didn't want to get too close to Stella again. Her vanilla scent was already burned into my nose, yet each time I was around it still made my brain whiteout.

Melody's eyes widened. "Alden? You're there too?"

"Yes."

"Oh, *interesting.*"

"There's nothing interesting here." Stella shook her head. "It's just two people who happened to be in the same place while Amma disappeared."

"Whatever you say, honey." But she had the same look Amma did whenever she didn't believe something we were saying. "So, Alden, you know how to handle this?"

"I do."

"We'll be fine," Stella insisted. "If the wind doesn't get us first."

"That old house always sounded terrifying in a storm," Melody said. "But it's strong. And you have someone experienced there."

"But turn your phones off to conserve power," her dad, Chris, said. "You won't be able to charge them, so save what you can if you need to call for help."

I could see Stella pale at the mention of calling for help.

"We'll save power, but we should be okay." I hoped my voice came out reassuring.

"You never know what will happen, especially since

there's snow coming afterward," Melody added. "I'm glad you're not alone, Stella. We were worried about you."

"I've got a fire going," I said. "And Amma made Stella stockpile some food. That won't last too long, considering the fridge won't stay cold forever, but Amma also has shelf-stable food. We'll be okay."

"Are you sure?"

"Yeah. I've done so many camping trips with less, even in the cold."

"All right, then. Stella, you have your survival buddy. No trying to get away from him—even if the roads look okay."

"I don't even have my car," she said. "Nick dropped me off."

"Where's your car?" Melody asked with a frown.

"Um, Nick was supposed to pick it up, but with the storm . . . I don't know."

"Pick it up from where?" Melody continued to frown.

"Reed's apartment." She lowered her voice as if she didn't want me to hear. I was too close to her for it to work. "I broke it off with him."

"Oh. What happened?"

"He proposed and I said no."

My eyes jerked to her. He *proposed*? Seconds later, I diverted my gaze, knowing Melody would catch my reaction.

I didn't need to let my feelings show. Unfortunately, I was bad at it when I was near Stella.

"I'm sorry, honey. Did you not see yourself with him forever?"

"No. I didn't even see myself with him through *Christmas.*"

"You'll find someone," Melody said. "And it might be good that you're away for a bit, then. It will be a good distraction."

Stella sighed. "Sure. Distraction by being stuck with ice. That was my first choice."

I huffed out a laugh. It had been far too long since I heard her sarcasm. She adopted a certain tone whenever it came out that never failed to make me smile.

"You've at least got Alden smiling," Melody said. "But you should have some fun, Stella. Take lots of pictures."

"I don't know if being in a snowstorm will be *fun.*"

"Fair. Maybe just try to stay alive, yeah?"

"Yeah, I'll try. I should go. My phone is only at thirty percent, and I should save the battery."

"Of course, honey. Be safe. Hopefully, you'll get power back soon. Stay warm, and don't let Reed get you down too much!"

She said her goodbyes and hung up. I resumed working, pretending I didn't hear anything.

"You have thoughts," she said. "I know you do."

"It's not really my place to share them."

"Yeah, but we're stuck together. We might as well get everything out in the open."

I pressed my lips together in an attempt not to talk

about her ex with her. It didn't work. "I just can't picture you engaged."

"Neither can I. It's why I said no."

"You couldn't see yourself marrying him but you were with him?"

"At one point, I *thought* it could work. He checked all the boxes. He had a fancy apartment and a good job. And he seemed to like me." Her eyes went to the window. "That's hard to find."

I opened my mouth to tell her she was so fucking wrong it wasn't even funny, but then I stopped myself. What the hell was I doing? Telling her that was opening a door I'd slammed shut years ago.

At least I still had a shred of control.

"Anyway," she said with a humorless chuckle, "I should have known it wouldn't work when he made shitty hot chocolate."

"Maybe that's how you should choose your boyfriends—how they make your favorite drink."

"Probably. But I don't know if I'll ever feel like being in a relationship. Even with Reed, it felt like a chore. I've never felt a connection with anyone, but . . ." Her eyes trailed to me and then back down to her phone. "Well, no one, I guess."

Silence stretched over us. Did she mean me? Had she felt it all those years ago too?

No. I didn't need to do this. I didn't need to think like this.

"I should go call my boss." I stood and took a few steps away from her.

"Yeah, you do that."

I threw on my coat and went outside, grateful for the frigid air. I didn't need to be out here, but I wanted to have some space. I never hated Nick more than I did whenever I was in Stella's orbit. I never wanted to *ruin* things with Nick more than I did now.

Running a hand through my hair, I called my boss who said that he could get to the park to help out the other ranger, Ryan, since he was in the city. He told me to stay safe and warm before hanging up.

And now that everything was taken care of in the outside world, it left me alone with Stella—something that I had no idea what to do about.

NINE

THOUGH ALDEN WASN'T EVEN in the house, I went to Amma's room for some time alone. But the second I sat on her bed, the cold seeped through my sweater and stayed there. I didn't know how Alden kept going outside and surviving.

I heard the front door open but I didn't move, still clinging to the hope that I could have some time alone. Soon, my hands grew cold and I had to move in search of the fire.

I shut the door and turned to Alden, who was once again checking on the stove. The first thing I noticed was the way his ass pressed into his dark-wash jeans. God, was it always so pert? What would it feel like to grab?

"Stella?" he asked as he turned. I averted my eyes.

"The bedrooms are freezing," I said as I shut the doors. "There's no way either of us could sleep in them."

"I figured that would happen. The living room is the

only livable room because of the fire." He went back to his work. "It's still our best option, but it creates a vacuum that sucks the heat out of the surrounding air."

"Huh. I didn't know that."

"Not many people do. They use fires for the looks, not . . . this."

"So, did you learn all of this stuff from your hikes?" I asked.

"That and being a park ranger."

"Right. You know, no one saw that coming."

"Neither did I. But I like it. Plus, it helps me keep you safe."

My skin prickled. I liked the idea of him keeping me safe—but I also wanted to take care of my own damn self.

The wind beat against the house again, reminding me just how scary this situation was. "I can't believe it got so bad so fast."

"It hit harder than they expected."

"That's not how storms usually go here. How many times did we see snowstorm warnings when we were kids and then be disappointed when they missed us? We always wanted school to be out for the day."

"I didn't like missing school."

"What? Why not?"

"School was the only place to get away from home. You and Nick made it bearable."

"I thought it was just Nick."

"No. You were always one of my favorite parts of school."

That feeling was back, the prickling one that turned my skin to gooseflesh. If anyone asked, I would say it was the cold.

But in reality, I *liked* hearing Alden talk like this.

"I'm glad you're happy," I said. "With your job and everything. It's all we wanted for you."

"And what about you? Are you happy?"

I stiffened as I considered it.

In some ways, I was. I liked capturing memories for people. I loved my best friend and my family.

But sometimes, at night, things felt *cold*. Even when I had been sharing a bed with someone.

"Yeah, of course." The lie felt thick, and I turned away. The camera was to my right, and I grabbed it, desperate for a distraction. "Smile!"

I got what was closer to a glare, but he still looked good in the photo after it was printed. Alden had a smolder I'd never seen before, especially when his gaze was directed at me.

"You're photogenic," I mumbled and handed him the photo.

"I look grumpy."

"I have a photographer's eye. You look fine."

"If you're behind the camera, who takes photos of you?"

"M-me?" I shook my head. "Not a lot of photos get taken of me."

He held out his palm. "Hand me the camera."

"I don't *need* photos of me. I know I don't look the

best—"

He raised an eyebrow as if daring me to complain about how I looked.

Winnie would give me one hell of a lecture for it, and I never would have done it had it not been for Reed.

Without another word, I handed him the camera.

Alden held it to his eye. "Turn to the right."

I did as I was told, expecting the photo to come out terrible.

It didn't.

Alden somehow knew the angle I usually used for selfies. My round face wasn't on full display and though I wasn't smiling, my eyes were filled with a fondness I didn't usually have.

And it was because of *who* I was looking at.

I cleared my dry throat. "You missed your calling."

"I take photos of people all the time at the park. And I knew your photo would turn out good."

I was thrown by his soft tone, feeling once again like the silly teenage version of me with a crush.

"We should figure out sleeping," I said, desperately needing to change the topic from me. "Will we share or—"

"I'll sleep in front of the fire on the floor. You take the couch." He said it so fast that I got the idea he didn't want me to finish my sentence.

"A-are you sure? The floor seems uncomfortable."

"I don't mind, and I highly doubt you'd want me to sleep on that tiny pullout couch mattress with you."

"A-absolutely not." I tried to sound convincing. But now my entire body was warm. As a teenager, I imagined what it would feel like for Alden's arms to be wrapped around me. I thought the closest I'd ever get was having him on top of me in the back of his truck.

"Thought so. There should be enough blankets to go around."

"Yeah, I'm sure it'll be fine."

* * *

WHEN I WOKE up only two hours later, I was shivering. The already near-zero temperature outside had dropped, and the living room felt like an icebox, somehow worse than the bedrooms were hours ago.

For a second, I thought about suffering and trying to force myself back to sleep, but then my cold hands reminded me that I literally couldn't.

"Alden," I whispered.

He didn't move at first and panic settled in.

What if he was dead? What the fuck would I do then?

"Alden!" I threw a pillow at him and he jerked awake.

He shot up faster than humanly possible.

"What?" he muttered in his low, rough sleep voice. My stomach flipped. I'd heard him like this when he'd stayed the night at our house, but the roughness of his voice had gotten lower with age. It did unfair things to my body.

And to make matters worse, his hair was adorably disoriented from sleep.

"Stella?" he urged, his voice growing worried. I shook myself out of my stupor.

"I think the fire went out."

He turned to the stove. "Fuck." He opened the door. It wasn't out, but it wasn't as warm as earlier. He cursed and poked it with a stick—something I didn't understand, and slowly, it came back to life.

But the cold had permeated the room. And it had to be even worse on the floor.

I knew the second that the thought crossed my mind that I would regret my next sentence.

But I was too cold to care.

"Get up here," I said.

"What?"

"This room is freezing."

"I'm fine."

"You have to be cold down there."

"I'm really not."

I got up and placed my hand on his. It was like an icicle.

He jerked it away seconds later. "What are you doing?"

"Calling you out on your lie. You're cold and it's worse on the floor. Get on the bed."

He considered it for far too long—so long I thought he would say no.

"Fine," he grumbled. He lay on the bed beside me,

sighing as if it were a chore. I closed my eyes. I could already feel his heat, and my entire body begged me to latch on to it.

I hated being cold. And sharing body heat was my thing. Many of my exes called me exceptionally clingy in my sleep, which didn't bode well for my pride. Reed even asked me to sleep in the guest room to break me of the habit. He didn't want me weighing him down.

Maybe Reed's dickish request was a good thing. I had gotten good at not cuddling on my nights alone. I could do it here too.

"Is it warming up?" he asked.

"Mostly."

His eyes met mine before he ripped them away.

"You really don't want to be up here, do you?" I asked.

"It's odd sharing a bed after not talking for seven years."

It was odder for me, considering he'd turned me down firmly all that time ago and my feelings were involuntarily rushing back.

"None of this is for fun," I muttered, unsure of who it was for, "it's just for survival."

The room was eerily silent except for the wind outside.

"Yeah," he said.

Silence returned, only broken by the shiver that racked my body.

"You're still cold?"

"I'll survive."

"Move closer."

"No."

Yes, my body begged.

"We should share heat."

I froze and then slowly turned to him. "What did you say?"

"Conserving heat. It's how we'll stay warm."

"I'm not cuddling with you."

"It's not cuddling. It's sharing heat. It's not . . . intimate. It's for survival."

Survival. I was starting to hate that word because despite everything, I did not want to be close to him only for survival.

TEN

"Do I really need to move?" Stella sounded like she was being tortured. "We're close enough as it is."

"We're not sharing heat here. Move closer."

"But—"

"Now."

"Since when are you so bossy?" She still didn't move.

"Come on. I said it didn't mean anything." And that was a lie. I'd be dreaming about this for the rest of my damn life. She'd be walking down the aisle, happy to be getting married to someone else, and this moment would play back in my mind.

"Cuddling isn't something that means *nothing* to me. Even if we don't talk anymore, I tend to . . . take it too far in my sleep."

"Take it too far?"

"I cling. A lot. And I'd rather freeze to death than do that with you."

I closed my eyes. She could never take it too far with me. Only I could with her.

"Don't worry. I won't ever bring it up again. What happens in this living room stays here."

"Really?"

"Yes."

It had to.

She shivered again. "Still no."

"I don't care about your pride. I'm not having you freeze to death in front of a fire."

"I'm not going to freeze to death. I'll just be miserable."

"I don't want that either."

Her only answer was silence. I took a chance, and I grabbed her by the waist, dragging her to me. She squeaked, her entire body tense as she finally got close enough to share my heat.

I threw the pile of warm, fuzzy blankets over us both.

"Fuck you for being warm."

"I'll try to be colder next time."

She breathed against my arm. My eyes closed as I took in every second of this feeling.

It had been seven years and three days since I'd had her this close. And yes, I'd kept track of each day, regret only piling on over time.

"Tell me again that this means nothing." Her voice was soft. I wondered if she'd gone down the rabbit hole I did.

I should have told her exactly what she wanted to hear.

But no words came out.

"Only you would fall asleep while holding me," she said darkly. "I guess I got my answer."

I stared at every strand of her hair and wished I *was* asleep. Her body's proximity and soft voice made me feel the things I swore I would never act on again.

But when she was this close, it was hard to remember the reasons why I swore not to.

Stella sighed, and her arm came around where mine was. "At least when you're asleep you won't let go."

I pressed my lips together to keep from saying that I'd never let go. I wouldn't have the first time if Nick hadn't made me.

Even now, he was going to murder me, but when Stella was here in my arms, I found that I didn't care all that much.

* * *

FORTUNATELY, I woke up first.

Or maybe it was very unfortunate.

Stella had only gotten closer, her legs now wound around mine. She had an iron grip on my arm, and her chest was pressed against me.

The plan was to move away. I stayed like a fool.

But then her breathing stuttered, and she jerked away.

"Fuck," she cursed. She turned to me, her cheeks dark red. "Of course you're awake."

"I said I wouldn't mention it."

"Then don't."

She was gone before I could say anything else, and I counted my lucky stars that she hadn't noticed that I was hard as hell.

My body never forgot how much it wanted her. I'd called this purely a survival-based, warmth-sharing session. Stella feeling my boner would raise some questions that I didn't know how to answer.

After I got up, I checked on the fire, stoking it back to life. Once the furnace was closed, I wandered into the kitchen, getting what I needed to make sure we had food and drink.

The fridge had held in a lot of its coolness, but I grabbed eggs and milk quickly, not wanting it to lose more than it needed to. I also grabbed Amma's cast-iron pan before making a second trip to get things to make coffee with.

"Are you a coffee drinker now?" I asked as I set down the final items in the living room.

"Is there a copious amounts of cream and sugar?"

"We can make something work."

"Then yes. How are you making it? I don't think a coffee machine will work without power."

"Hot water and a French press. This stove is for more than keeping the house warm."

"Since when does Amma have a French press?"

"I got it for her a while ago."

Stella watched silently as I worked. The water warmed and then I poured it over the coffee grounds. I checked the clock on the wall and gave it three minutes to brew. Once it was done, I handed her a mug. "Here."

Her cheeks turned pink. "Thanks. What is all of the rest for?"

"I'm making eggs. Or attempting to."

"I'll make them," she offered. "You'll destroy the cast-iron pan if you don't use it right. Hand it over."

I got out of the way as she took over the warm pan, cracking the eggs into the skillet. She mixed milk and butter into it, creating a fluffy scramble for us both.

"Good work," I said.

"You haven't tasted it yet."

"You made it, so I know it's good."

She smiled under the praise, making me wonder if her idiot of an ex ever said anything like this to her at all. How could he have had a woman like her and messed it up? How did he not see her for what she was?

Stella sat across from me and took a bite of her eggs. "Fuck," she nearly moaned. "It's been too long since I had good eggs."

"Let me guess, Reed didn't eat egg yolks."

"You'd be right. Cholesterol, I think. He didn't have a problem but thought he could in the future." She shuddered. "I went months without eggs, and even sugar."

"How did you survive that?"

"I snuck some in when things got desperate."

I could see Stella with contraband stuffed into her purse. "That reminds me of the time you snuck in brownies in high school."

"Oh, when Nick lied to me and didn't tell me they were pot brownies? I could have gotten arrested for that."

"I doubt—"

"Could you see me in prison? Be honest, Alden."

"I would have bailed you out."

She rolled her eyes, a smile playing on her lips. "There you go again, covering for Nick even in the hypothetical. He needs to own up for his own shit and bail me out himself."

I didn't have anything to say to her. She'd struck a little too close to home, and the memory of me telling her that we wouldn't work to cover for his discomfort played behind my eyes.

Luckily, her eyes were now on the stove.

"Will you teach me how to keep the fire going?"

"Why?"

"It's something I should know. Besides, I can't let you do all the work."

"I'm happy to do all the work."

"Then I'm not the kind of woman to let a guy do everything for her. And if you die because you're outside splitting logs, then I'll need to survive somehow."

"I'm not going to die because I'm splitting some logs."

"Oh, then how *will* you die?"

My eyes moved to her. I had a feeling *she* would be the death of me.

And it would be the greatest end I could ask for.

"Nothing," I said. "I'm immortal."

She rolled her eyes. It almost felt like we were kids again, getting along. "I still want to know how to take care of the fire. I need something to do with all of this time."

"Keeping a fire going isn't going to take all day."

"Don't remind me. The boredom is already eating me alive." Her eyes went to the window, gazing over the white scenery. Everything was brighter than I'd ever seen. The sun wasn't yet out and more flurries dumped from the sky. Hollywood would have a hard time crafting a winter wonderland as perfect as this one.

I let out a sigh when I looked at it.

"That's gonna be a nightmare for everyone," I said lowly. After years of working in parks, I had yet to see a storm like this, but even the smaller ones over the years had been a logistical nightmare.

She turned to me. "Do you remember when we got three inches of snow back when we were all in school? You, Nick, and I went out to the park, and Mom thought we were missing?"

"You guys got the lecture of your life." I cracked a smile. "But it was fun. Watching Nick eat shit always is."

"There are good hills here. And Amma has sleds in the shed."

"It's a little cold."

"We have a fire."

I didn't know how to answer her. I *wanted* to go, but I knew that the walls I'd built around us were cracking.

But then she sighed at my silence. "Never mind."

I turned to find her curled into herself, looking as sad as she had when I first saw her again.

All of my control went out the window. I was *not* going to be the one who made her feel like this. Fuck no.

"We'll go. If you were inviting me, that is."

"Who else is around?" she asked. "And if I go alone, it's no fun."

"So, let's do it. The sleds are in the shed?"

"Yeah."

"Good." I got up and threw her my jacket.

"I'm not—"

"If we're doing this, you're staying warm. And my jacket is the best option you have."

Her nose crinkled. "But—"

"Wear my jacket, Stella."

She rolled her eyes as she put it on. "I'm only doing this because it's cold. You're getting this back when all of this is over."

"Sure, whatever makes you feel better." I didn't know if I could take it back. It would smell like her, and I would be stuck with the memory of this time we had together.

"I only hope that this time it's *you* who falls on your ass," she said as she put on gloves.

"That's a rude thing to say. And besides, you're not

allowed to make fun of me. What happens in the snow, stays in the snow, remember?"

Her lips curled into a smile. "That only counts in the living room. And you embarrassing yourself? No way in hell I'm forgetting that."

ELEVEN

THE WIND WAS BRUTAL, but climbing up the hill was even more so. Out here, I could see why we weren't allowed to leave. It made me wonder why Alden kept choosing to go outside rather than stay in.

"You surviving back there?" he asked as we got to the top.

"For the record," I gasped out, "I always took the stairs at Reed's apartment."

"I'm pretty sure that's different than climbing a hill."

"Still. I work out, even if I don't look like I do."

He paused. "Does that mean what I think it means?"

"What?"

"That you're tying physical weight to your health?"

"I mean, I know it doesn't matter, but so many guys think it does."

"I'm not most guys."

"Are you not?"

"Definitely not. I've seen people double my size run up mountains. Every body is different, including yours."

"Sure, but I'm *walking* up a hill gasping for breath."

"Stella, it's nearly zero degrees and windy. Give yourself some grace."

"You seem fine."

"I do this kind of thing every day," he replied. "Come to my park after this, and you'll see why I'm not sweating."

"Yeah, right. I highly doubt you want me to go to your park."

"I wouldn't mind you there." He turned to look at me, eyebrow raised.

Flecks of snow dotted his dark hair. His five-o'clock shadow was more visible now, darkening the lower half of his face. Neither of us said anything, but I could feel impossible heat in his stare. My heart skipped a beat.

"S-so, ready to go down the hill?" An awkward chuckle followed my question.

"You're really avoiding the park thing."

"We came out here to sled, not talk about meeting up after this." I gestured down the hill. "Your turn."

"You go first."

"No. You."

"We could both go at the same time."

"But then how will I see you fall on your ass?"

He shook his head. "Fine. I'll go first. But you have to ask nicely."

I fluttered my eyelashes at him. "Pretty please?"

I thought he would roll his eyes and get into position. Instead, his breath stuttered and he stared at me with parted lips. A shiver rolled down my spine.

"What? You said to ask nicely." When he didn't respond, I swatted at my face. "Do I have snow stuck to me or something?"

"N-no. I just forgot what it was like when you acted *nice*."

"Very funny."

Alden's eyes finally slid from me, and he put down his sled.

"All right," he said, blowing out a breath. It was visible in the frigid temperatures. "Here goes nothing."

He started out strong, his speed steady. But then he suddenly moved the wrong way and flipped over with a loud, "Fuck!"

I covered my mouth to keep a laugh from bubbling out of me.

See, my kryptonite was people falling. It was a terrible habit, but there was something about a wipeout that brought me pure joy. I managed to keep my amusement inside, but only barely.

"Are you okay?" I called out.

"I'm fine. You can laugh now."

Once I heard that, I lost it.

I hadn't laughed this hard in years, but Alden was always so put together. He was my big brother's best friend, always above me somehow.

But the snow reduced him into a pile on the ground.

Slowly, he got up. "You gonna go, or what?"

"Fine," I called back. "But if I fall, you can't laugh."

"That doesn't seem fair."

"Life isn't fair," I said as I got on the sled.

Because of the ice, I went *much* faster than I thought I would. I could see what tripped up Alden—a dip in the ground—and I was able to avoid it, though barely.

"I survived!" I yelled as I finally slowed down.

"Lucky you. My hip hates you."

"Let's do it again."

"I might die."

"I thought you were immortal," I mocked.

"Not when you're around."

"At least you'll have fun if you meet your end." I grabbed his arm. "Come on. I'll race you to the top."

I took off without waiting for a response.

"Stella!" he groaned. "I'm still recovering."

"So I'll have a chance of beating you!" I called back, a laugh escaping me. Moments later, I heard snow crunching and saw him catching up. He beat me to the top, like I knew he would, but I didn't regret the race.

"Best two of three?" I asked.

"Survive the trip down first," he said. "Your turn."

"I just went."

"I want to see the view from up here this time."

I rolled my eyes but threw the sled into the snow. I flew down the hill with a smile on my face.

And as I reached the bottom, it hit me that I felt like myself for the first time in years.

* * *

"T-THAT WAS FUN," I said as I took off my soggy jacket. I shivered from the temperature, but even that couldn't stop my grin.

"It was." Alden was at the fire again, making sure it was burning.

"S-shouldn't you be cold too?"

"I am, but you're still smaller than me."

"I'm—" I paused when he stood at his full height.

Okay. Maybe he was.

"You're not *that* much taller than me."

"Whatever makes you feel better."

The cool hair hit my neck and I shivered again. "I can't get warm."

"Sweater off," Alden said, seriousness in his tone. "Pants too."

The order would have been sexy if it hadn't been for the fact that I was freezing. "I'll go to Amma's room."

"It's ten degrees colder in there."

My pride shivered too. "Fine. Then turn around."

He threw me a new set of clothes and did as I asked. I made quick work of changing. I threw on my extra leggings and a T-shirt. I wished I had another sweater, but Nick had packed the bag, and I was pretty sure he simply shoved things in just like he had the night he picked me up.

"I'm done," I said. "Now throw me into the fire like a log."

"Not happening. Nick would kill me."

I huddled close to the furnace, almost touching it. I heard shuffling, and I turned, only to see Alden shirtless.

"Oh my God," I said, jerking my eyes away before I could stare, but the memory of tanned skin stuck out in my mind.

It hit me that I hadn't seen him shirtless, even when we slept together.

"What?" he asked.

My eyes trailed his tanned, toned skin. "Nothing, sorry."

Even after all of these years, I was still attracted to him. That flash of skin was all it took to make me want him.

I stared at the stove as if it had personally offended me.

"Feeling better?" he asked.

Not emotionally, but physically . . . "Yes."

And then another shiver hit me.

"You're lying."

"How about we talk about the real issues, like why you're shirtless?"

"My clothes got wet."

"Amma might have some of her ex's stuff."

"I'll look in a few minutes. I'm more worried about if you're still cold."

Fuck. He can't be shirtless and then care about me too. It was too much.

"I'm not."

"We could share heat again."

My mouth went dry. I played it as cool as possible, but our first instance of sharing heat was almost too much to handle. I'd forgotten why I hated him the second more than an inch of his body touched mine.

And this time there would be far more of us touching.

"Just put me into the fire."

"Like I said, not an option. Just touch me."

His voice was hard, reminding me that he didn't like this any more than I did.

This was probably his worst nightmare.

Another shiver racked my body as he sat next to me.

"Just for survival," he reminded. I gritted my teeth and leaned into him, forcing myself to not fully melt into the heat of his arms.

His skin was warm as it pressed against mine. His hands were only a touch less cold than mine as they wound around my back.

Just for survival. Not fun.

But my body didn't get the memo. It latched onto every sensation, cementing it into my memory.

His body hair, as dark as the hair on his head, tickled my skin, and I couldn't deny that I was heating up fast.

My arms snaked around him, pulling him closer. I trained my ears on him, ready to hear him groan in annoyance.

Instead, I heard him swallow.

I liked this. I shouldn't, yet I did.

Alden pulled me in closer.

This shouldn't be intimate. This was for a purpose, yet my fast-beating heart wondered if I could take it further. Could I scoot into his lap and sit on his strong thighs? Could I nuzzle into his neck and feel his beard tickle my cheek?

I stayed rooted to the spot as seconds turned into minutes, not daring to ruin it.

He cut the contact first.

"We should be good now," he said, standing. He threw his shirt over his head.

"Isn't that still wet?"

"Yeah, but I need to cool off anyway."

Silence rained down on us, and I wondered if there was a string of words I could use to get him to come back to me again.

But I didn't think I could take another no from him.

"So what else do we do?" I asked.

He considered it. "Want to do a puzzle?"

I blinked. "What?"

"Puzzles are one of your Christmas traditions. We can keep some of them, right?"

It was a sweet gesture, and while the warmth of him still lingered on my skin, it made my stomach twist. "Yeah, maybe we can."

TWELVE

We pulled out an old Christmas puzzle, one with a classic Santa on it. The Summers had done it a million times, and the faint smile on Stella's face told me I'd chosen the right one.

"It's a shame that we don't have any music," she said as we distributed the pieces on the dining room table. "Christmas puzzles are incomplete without it."

The world felt off after I'd pulled her close. Instead of caring about my goal to stay away from her, I thought of everything I could do to make her smile. I should have excused myself to another room to give her space, to give *me* space. Instead, I stood, looking for something to make music for her.

I found one of Amma's antique snow globes on the side table. It was of kids playing in a scenic village. On the bottom was a tab to wind it to play music.

"Here," I said, gently setting it on the table. "This isn't the same, but it works."

"I haven't seen this thing in forever," she said. "Does it still work?"

I wound it up and a simple version of "Frosty the Snowman" played.

"It's better than nothing."

I was rewarded with a grateful smile as I set it back down. "This helps."

Her eyes fell to the puzzle, and I couldn't help but think about the hug again. I needed to stop, but every moment I got to touch her was all that was on my mind.

Slowly, she separated all of the edge pieces. She and Amma had always been organized by their puzzle building while Nick and I worked on the easy-to-connect pieces, like Santa's face. Nick was abysmally bad at them, so I usually handed him pieces that went together.

Stella and I had always been the ones who were the most efficient, but this time I didn't reach for any pieces. I was too busy thinking of her.

"You gonna help me?" she asked. "I can do this by myself, but it's more fun when I don't have to piece together the center."

"Yeah, sorry. I got distracted."

She glanced up at me and our eyes met. For a second, we only stared. Then she broke the contact and went back to the puzzle. I followed suit.

She had half the edge down within ten minutes, and I had the sled built in the same amount of time.

I was pulled out of my concentration when she snapped a photo. "This is a calm moment," she said. "It'll be nice to remember."

"My hands might ruin the shot."

She glanced at them and looked back at the developing photo. "No, I think it will be fine. The photo is turning out great."

I didn't know how hands could look great at all, but I didn't question her.

"Is it this quiet where you live?" she asked after we lapsed back into silence.

"Sometimes. It's still a park, so every now and then, someone's rowdy, but oftentimes it's just nature and the occasional hiker."

"It's nice. I've lived downtown for the last two years, and it's so loud sometimes."

"Living in the city always drained me."

"I thought I liked it, but everything felt *gray* after a lot of it. Being here feels right."

"You're feeling better?"

"Not all the way. I'm still a little sad about wasting two years of my life with Reed. But I'm finding things to take photos of again, and I'm laughing too. I didn't realize it then, but I gave up way too much of myself while with him. And when the usual comments started, it only got worse."

"What usual comments?"

"About how I'm too much. About how I dress or how I act. He's the fourth guy in a row who I was a problem for."

"*Fourth?*"

Her eyes drifted up to me. "Don't act so shocked. I'm sarcastic, loud, and colorful—at least when I'm myself. It's not exactly what people are looking for in a long-term partner."

I could only stare. How could someone look at someone as bright as her and call her *too much*? How could they ever ask her to change a single fucking thing about herself when she was already so damn perfect?

"Let me guess," she said at my silence, "you think they're right too."

"They're fucking *wrong.*"

Her eyes grew wide. "But—"

"Stella, you're exactly how you should be. Never change for some fucking idiot who doesn't realize what he has."

"So, you didn't turn me down because of how I am?"

"What? *No.*"

"Oh. I thought . . . I thought I was annoying."

"No. You were never the problem. It was me. Always me."

The words hung heavy in the air, and I could only hope that she believed them.

"So it wasn't my personality or my clothes or—"

"It was never any of that. You don't have to change a

thing. For every person who doesn't like you, another will love you exactly as you are."

"And which side are you on?"

What a dangerous question. I knew I couldn't answer it.

"Be yourself. Don't stay around people who change you."

Stella's shoulders slumped. I knew that wasn't the answer she wanted. It was the right one—it had to be, though it didn't feel like it.

Getting trapped with her was one of the worst things because as time went on, the memory of why I was doing this kept fading.

"I don't hate you," I added. "I could never hate you."

"You just can't *date* me."

"Could *you* date me? After everything?"

She was going to say no—she had to.

If she didn't, I didn't know what I would do.

"It's just a hypothetical. After my string of awful luck, it would be nice to know that *someone* wants me."

Don't say anything. For the love of God, keep your mouth shut.

"Someone *does* want you. I can promise you that."

Her green eyes met mine again. Years could have passed in that moment, but it didn't matter. The intensity of her gaze spoke volumes.

I want it to be you, I could have sworn she was saying.

It could have just been my feelings manifesting. It could have been that she was staring *at me* and not behind me. But I wanted her to say those words. I wanted to know that I could still mean something to her.

Even if I didn't deserve it.

"Yeah, maybe." Her eyes fell back down to the puzzle and she went silent. My shoulders slumped. It should have been a relief that she didn't tell me she still wanted me.

It wasn't.

THIRTEEN

WE FINISHED the puzzle by the time the day gave into night. My focus was purely on the pieces in front of me because I couldn't look at Alden anymore.

He wasn't a teenage crush. He was a forever crush, always in my periphery. Except now, he was right in front of me, and I literally couldn't leave. I wished I were the type of woman to get hurt and never like a man again.

Instead, I was a glutton for pain.

As the night's cold air seeped into the house, I found an extra sweater to layer on and huddled under the blanket that was thrown on the pullout couch. I was not built for this kind of never-ending cold.

"Already going to sleep?" Alden asked.

"Maybe I will once I finally feel warm again."

The space between his eyebrows creased and he

checked the fire. It was still burning bright, giving us blessed warmth.

"Get up here," I said.

He slowly turned, an eyebrow raised. "You say that like you're about to murder me."

"I'm tired of needing you for warmth. And I'm tired of you being warm. It's unfair."

"You could just be tired of *me*."

"Are you tired of me?"

He looked back at the fire. "You can tell me to fuck off, you know. There aren't a lot of places to go, but I'd make it work."

I didn't miss his diversion. Maybe admitting it would make it harder for the both of us.

"You'd freeze anywhere else but here."

"Seems like a small price to pay for everything I've done."

What a line. With him saying things like that, it was no wonder my crush never went away.

"It's fine," I replied. "You don't need to pay a price."

"But you don't need to be miserable."

"We're stuck in my grandmother's house during the snowstorm of the century. It's going to be miserable."

"The situation can be, but not you. Or at least not you when I'm the one causing it."

"But you *have* caused me misery."

The room went silent for a long time.

"Yeah," he said with a sigh. "I have."

"Do you regret it?"

"Every day, Stella."

My heart skipped a beat. I couldn't stop thinking of *what if?*

What if he'd given us a shot?

What if he liked me?

What if it had worked out for once?

I turned away from him.

"Stella—"

"I'm going to sleep."

"But—"

"We don't have to talk about it. I'm fine."

"You're not fine."

"What do you want me to say, Alden?" I snapped, turning to him. "This is the story of my life. I like a guy, and he either wants to change me or pushes me away. After a while, it wears you down."

"Don't you remember what I said? It was *never* you."

"Yeah, sure. It wasn't me, but it still ended the same way. With me alone."

"You should have *never* been alone. You're Stella Summers—the most beautiful woman on the *planet*. Your smile is fucking heavenly and the sound you make when you laugh is better than any song I've ever heard. And any man should have seen that from day one."

My jaw dropped. I had to be floating in dreamland because there was no way he just said any of that to me.

"And you did?" My voice was barely above a whisper.

Color drained from his face. "I . . . You're my friend. Of course I did."

I crashed back down to Earth.

"Friend," I repeated. "Right."

The idea of staying friends when he'd just compli-mented me like *that* seemed impossible. But I had to live with what he offered me. Dreaming of more had never worked out for me.

"Stella, I—"

"Don't apologize," I said. "I get it. Friends is what you want, and that's what you'll get."

I wanted more. I always would. But I could live with this being enough.

"Are you still cold?" he asked as he lay down too.

"Yeah. I'm just sensitive to the cold."

"You've always been cold-natured."

"We could huddle for warmth again. That's what friends would do, right?"

"If it's dire, yes."

It wasn't. I probably could survive even if the tip of my nose was cold. "Is this a dire situation?"

"I'd say so."

"Okay, then we can huddle."

I scooted closer to him, and his body heat immedi-ately sank into me. Fuck. He was like a heater.

"I hate that you're so warm."

"Yeah, yeah." His arm came to rest around me and it felt like the most natural thing in the world. "Maybe once you get some rest, you'll smile again."

"Need some heaven?" I asked.

He huffed out a laugh. "I'm not living that one down, am I?"

"Nope. Never. And you didn't answer my question."

"Fine. I do. It's been a long time since I've seen you smile. And the more I do, the more I *want* to."

* * *

THE MORNING LIGHT filtered through the living room windows. I came to consciousness slowly, the unusual brightness nearly blinding. Snow still fell from the sky, though slower than the day before. I thought about Amma, stuck with her neighbor, and I hoped she was okay.

Alden was behind me, sound asleep. His arm was tight around me as if I would float away. His chest was warm against my back, and for once, I wasn't freezing. I felt warm and safe.

Cuddling with him was better for my sleep than I wanted to admit. This was the first time in a long time that I felt truly rested. His touch banished any lingering cold, and I could easily get used to waking up like this every day.

I wished he felt the same way.

I was about to extract myself from his warm hold, but then all thoughts flew out of my mind when his hips rolled forward.

He was hard. So, so hard. And his erection was pressing right into my inner thighs.

Right where I wanted him.

I didn't let myself think of my first time very much. While it had been amazing, the days after had hurt. But now I couldn't help but flash back to it.

It had been *so* good. So much better than all of my exes.

After seven years of mediocre sex, the memory of Alden fucking me was welcome. Maybe I'd talked it up in my mind, but the way no man could compare had weighed on me over the years. Missionary and a bland orgasm nowhere near the ones from Alden weren't enough.

But I didn't need to think this way. We were friends. *Just* friends. The friction meant nothing.

"Damn it, Stella," Alden said from behind. "You don't know what you do to me."

I blinked. What the hell? I thought he didn't want me.

Just as I opened my mouth to ask, he rolled away and disappeared to the bathroom.

I stayed rooted to the spot, trying and failing to make sense of what had just happened.

He was right about one thing, I supposed; I didn't know what I had done to him.

Friends wouldn't say anything like that. Romance aside, he wanted *me*, or at the very least, my body.

Maybe he was in a dry spell, but I doubted it. Alden always had his choice of women. It was one of the things that drove me crazy when we were teens. I doubted it changed now.

I shook off my thoughts and went to the kitchen. The fridge wasn't cool anymore, which meant most of the food inside had gone bad, but I found muffins to munch on while I figured out my next move.

I wanted to ask him about it, but I had no idea how. I was still working on it when he came out of the bathroom a few minutes later. His dark hair was wet, curling into his neck. His skin was prickled with gooseflesh.

"Did you take a shower in the cold?"

"I needed it," was all he said.

I looked down at myself, knowing I probably needed one too.

"How awful was the cold water?" I asked.

"Not bad." He wasn't looking me in the eye, and I wondered if he'd had his fill of me. Maybe it was time for me to shower too.

"Guess it's my turn," I said, getting up.

"Stella, wait. Maybe you should—"

"It's fine. I need a minute to myself anyway."

When I was alone in the bathroom, I gave myself one breath to think more about what had happened on the pullout couch. Then I put it out of my mind and turned on the water.

I nearly yelped when I felt the frigid water. Alden had to be lying. There was no way this shower wasn't going to be *terrible*.

I considered skipping it, but one smell of my pits told me I absolutely couldn't. It had to happen, and I had to be miserable.

And it was. The water pelted me with unrelenting cold. This was my worst nightmare, and my hands turned to ice within the first minute. I washed myself as fast as I could, thankful I'd left a bottle of my favorite body wash here when I stayed over a few weeks ago to get a break from Reed.

When I turned off the water, I was racked with full-body shivers and all I wanted to do was find whatever warmth I could. I dried off as fast as my stiff hands would let me, but clothes didn't seem to help at all. My wet hair went into a towel, and I cursed everything from the weather to the shit luck that had gotten me here.

I even cursed the invention of the water heater. Maybe I would have been used to cold water if I'd never known the luxury of a hot shower.

The living room was warmer, but it wasn't enough.

"Y-you said it wasn't that bad," I stuttered out. I sat in front of the fire, trying to move my hands.

"Are you okay?"

"Do I *look* okay?"

He was wearing an old flannel, one of Amma's ex's if I had to guess, but as much as I wanted to admire how it stretched over his muscular arms, I was too miserable to.

"Come here," he said.

"You're not gonna touch me after a betrayal like that."

"It wasn't that bad for *me*, but you're cold-natured. It won't happen again."

It definitely wouldn't because I was never showering in the cold again.

His offer was tempting. And not only because he was a living heater. I was growing far too used to the feeling of his body pressed against mine.

"F-fine." I let him sit next to me on the couch. He pulled me to him and I sank into his warmth. I pressed my face into his chest, eager to be as close as possible.

I could hear his heartbeat. It galloped a mile a minute, and I wondered if it was because *I* was near.

Something wasn't adding up, and as much as I wanted to enjoy being friends with him again, I needed to know *why* he acted the way he did and why his body told an opposite story.

"Feeling better?"

His voice was different when I was so close to him. It sent shock waves through my body.

"Yeah, a little."

"Good. I need to go chop some wood."

Alden was gone without another word. I replaced his warmth with a blanket, and I sighed in the empty living room.

"Alden Canes, what the fuck is going on?"

Boredom eventually weighed heavy on me and I found myself missing my phone. I didn't realize how much I used it until I didn't have it.

After I felt sufficiently warmed, I searched for the only technology that worked—Amma's Polaroid. At first, I took a picture of the roaring flames inside the stove and the bed we'd made. Then I glanced outside at where

Alden was chopping wood. It was in perfect view of the dining room window.

And *that* was a picture-worthy sight. Now that I was alive again, I could finally see how hot he looked. I snapped a few shots and waited for them to develop before shoving them into my bag. I would keep those for later.

But as I watched him again, I realized how therapeutic chopping the wood must be. It seemed way better than sitting inside like a loser.

I checked to be sure my hair was dry before bundling up in Alden's jacket and some gloves. I walked outside into frigid air and took a moment to look around the land. Off in the distance, I could barely see the main road, and it looked as pristine as Amma's driveway—it was obvious no one had driven on it, and I couldn't blame them with all the hills.

It hit me just how lucky I was to have someone with me who knew how to survive. Alden was a blessing, and while it had been rough at first, I knew I couldn't have done this without him.

"What are you doing out here?" he asked, brow furrowed at the sight of me.

"I want to join in on your therapy session."

"My what?"

"Your wood chopping. Sure, it's for survival, but it also looks like a great way to get anger out."

"Are you angry?"

"I'm feeling emotions. Can I try my hand at it?"

He handed over the axe. I swung it over my head, only for it to stick in the wood, getting me nowhere.

"Huh. Maybe I'm not good at this type of therapy."

"Here," he said, taking the axe from me. "Let me show you. You have to angle it for the weakest part of the wood and clench your abs when you swing." He threw down the axe. "See how I did it?"

"You make it look easy."

And hot.

"I had to practice. Try again."

"No, I think one failure is enough."

"I'd like to see your strength for once."

"How do you know I'm strong?"

"You're Stella Summers." He said it like it was obvious, just like he had when he'd called me the most beautiful woman on the planet.

All of the compliments did more than I wanted to admit. Most of all, it empowered me.

I brought the axe up, but stopped when he walked over. "Hang on," he said lowly, "your angle is off."

"Show me again."

He moved closer, his gloved hands coming over mine to adjust the axe. I gulped, not used to him casually being so close. "There."

"Help me mimic the swing?" I asked.

I felt his breath on my cheeks as he sighed, but he moved to where he was behind me. "You swing it like this."

His arms guided mine, and I swore I could feel his

warmth through our jackets. I barely caught on to what he was showing me because I was too busy feeling him be close to me when we *weren't* huddling to stay warm.

"Okay, I think I have it." My words were soft. My body couldn't take more of this torture—not when he wouldn't be touching me at the end of it.

Alden stepped away. "Go for the middle of the wood."

"Bold of you to assume I can aim."

He laughed. "You can do anything."

I bit my lip but brought down the axe. It split perfectly in half.

"I did it!" I said, throwing my hands in the air.

"Can you do it again?"

His subtle challenge made me bring the axe up again. As it came down, I thought of all the things that had pissed me off. Reed. My confusion about Alden. This damn snowstorm. All were hacked away with the bits of wood.

"You weren't kidding," he said. "You had stuff to work out."

"Been a rough few days." I handed the axe back to him. "Now I see how you survive out here. Chopping wood warms you up."

"A little. It's also nice to be outside."

"And hey, if you love it too much and freeze, now I can survive without yo—whoa!" I fell on my ass in the snow as I walked over to him. There was a moment of mortifying silence before he burst into laughter.

"Oh, Stella. Never change."

"Don't patronize me."

"Hey, you laughed your ass off when I went sledding. We're just even now."

I raised my hand to flip him off. The cold was infecting me again. "I hate this."

"Need some help getting up?"

"Just fucking carry me back," I groaned. I was mostly kidding, but when he hauled me onto his back, I squeaked. "You don't have to—"

"It's fine."

"What if you fall too?"

"I won't. I have something important to protect this time."

I was shocked into silence.

He might not fall, but I sure as fuck was going to. But it was in a much more dangerous way.

FOURTEEN

"So you stoke it like this." I showed Stella how to poke the fire and roar it back to life. It was hours later, and we'd been busy doing other puzzles as the fire died.

She was the one to notice it was going out, and she darted to grab the metal poker before I'd even gotten up. She looked so excited to learn that I knew I wouldn't say no.

"Okay, so chopping wood, stoking fires. Is there anything else about survival I need to know?"

"Why, are you trying to kick me out into the cold?"

"No." She rolled her eyes. "It's just nice to learn new things again. My life had become a slog of one thing after another, and everything was set into place. I'm happy it's different, even if we're stuck here for who knows how long. What day is it anyway?"

"It's Christmas Eve."

"Really?" Her eyes trailed to the window where everything was still icy. It was dark now, but we could still see it reflect against the dim light of the moon. "Damn. I guess there really isn't a chance of getting out of here by tomorrow."

"No, I don't think so."

Stella blew out a breath. "It doesn't even feel like the holiday without the lights. Santa is out right now, and I feel like it's any other day."

"There's no way you still believe in Santa, right?"

She laughed. "Of course I don't. But sometimes I like to believe in the magic."

"The Summers always have a magical Christmas, Santa or not. It's far better than what mine were at home."

"You never even wanted to be home back then."

"Why be home when I have you guys? My dad didn't even let me believe in Santa."

Her eyes widened. "What? Why?"

"He thought it was all a ploy to get us to buy more for the holiday."

"To be fair, it is. But it's still magical sometimes to remember when things were easier."

"I'm glad you have those memories."

"I mean, you have them too. In a different way. You were welcome every year. I like to think we also tried to make your Christmases special."

And they were. Every single one of them. This family had saved me, and I would never be able to pay them back for that.

And it all started when I was assigned to sit next to the happy-go-lucky popular boy in my grade.

"Every day I'm glad I met Nick," I said softly.

The reminder of Nick hit me hard. I needed to remember what I owed him—what he'd asked me to do. The dull ache I was used to when around the Summers, and especially when near Stella, was a sharp pain now. I'd spent too much time with her.

But I needed to get over it. This was how friendship went. Sometimes it hurt, but I got to keep my connection to the Summers family.

"Alden?" she asked. "Are you okay? You got lost in thought."

I looked over at her. Her hair fell over her shoulders in waves and the open door of the fire made her face glow. God, she'd only gotten more beautiful over the years, and I knew she would continue to.

One day, she would find the perfect man. One that wasn't her brother's best friend.

Yet now, after spending all of this time with her, the thought filled me with a miserable feeling that added to the sharp pain in my chest. I didn't want her with anyone else. I wanted her with *me*.

Even if I didn't deserve it. Even if I would blow up my life to do it.

"Yeah, I'm good."

"Sometimes you look at me and go quiet."

"It's nothing."

"Does it have to do with what happened seven years ago?"

I looked up at her, eyes wide. "We don't need to talk about it."

"Friends talk about their problems."

"I . . . *still*."

Her lips pursed and she stoked the fire again. "Do you want an apology?"

I looked at her, incredulous. "For *what*?"

"Me coming on to you."

"No, I don't need an apology for any of it. If anything, I owe you one. I should have said no."

She looked at me, eyes narrowed. "So you regret it."

"No," I said before I could stop myself.

"Then, *why—*"

"Don't. Let's forget this conversation."

"But—"

"Stella."

"Alden," she snapped. "We need to talk about this."

"There's nothing to talk about."

"Is there not? Because just this morning you said I didn't know what I did to you."

I sucked in a breath. I'd been sure she was still fast asleep, none the wiser of how much I wanted her.

"That was . . ."

She scoffed. "What? You have nothing to say to my face?"

I had nothing *good* to say to her face.

But she wasn't going to let me get away with that.

"Well?"

She was challenging me in the way only she could, spice with a dash of vulnerability.

And I could never lie. Not seven years ago and certainly not now.

"I did say that."

"So you want me. Physically, that is."

The flames flickered, and I caught sight of her neck in the light. I had to rip my eyes away before I broke like last time.

"The world doesn't end if you admit it," she added.

Mine could, yet no lies could escape me. "You're right. About me wanting you physically."

Her eyes went back to the fire. "Then would you want to act on it?"

"What?" I asked. "Act on it as in . . ."

"Be physical again. Nothing romantic. I just got out of a bad relationship, and you would never want one with me. So we can be casual."

Casual. There was nothing casual about my feelings for her. They were all-consuming, infecting every inch of me.

"No," I said.

Stella's brow furrowed. "Why not?"

"Because you deserve something more than casual."

Her mouth opened and then shut. She was quiet for a moment before she said, "Then we can be more than casual."

"No. That's even worse."

"Let me guess, because I'm me and you're you."

"Because you deserve someone else. Someone better. Not me."

Her brow creased. "Why do you get to decide what I deserve?"

"Because I see you for the perfection that you are. I broke your heart, Stella. Hold me accountable for that."

"Are you sorry?"

"Of course I am."

"Will you do it again?"

"I . . . I don't want to ever do that again."

Which is why I needed to put a stop to this now.

But she was wearing that goddamn teal color again. It was a different sweater, but it was still the perfect color on her. She was ethereal in this light, just like she had been all those years ago.

She moved closer, just by an inch. Her eyes were on my lips and my breath caught at the idea of her kissing me again.

I put my hands on her shoulders before this could go any further.

"Stella, don't." It came out like a growl. My will was hanging on by a thread.

Her eyes met mine, a devious smile on her lips. "You keep saying things that don't match your actions. So I think it's time that I stop listening."

Her hands gripped my flannel, bringing me in closer. "Goddammit," I groaned.

"Do you want me to stop?" she asked, eyes moving to mine.

And when I was faced with the only green I'd seen in days, I was powerless. "Fuck no."

"I knew it," she said. Her lips closed over mine, filling me with the vanilla scent that once followed me like a ghost.

But here it was real. She was in front of me, stealing my breath with one simple kiss.

And all the fight left me.

Fuck it. I wanted her.

My body flickered back to life, finally escaping the seven-year slumber. We were only inches apart, but that was too far. My hands went to her waist, dragging her the remaining distance until she was practically in my lap.

Our tongues clashed and I suddenly couldn't catch my breath.

I could feel her smile into my mouth. Fuck, she already knew she had a hold on me.

Stella's hands wrapped around my neck and she pulled me on top of her. I braced her with my forearms, lowering my body to where I had the contact I desperately needed.

The pain disappeared, pushed away by her body touching mine. Things felt right for once, like a puzzle piece slotting into place.

I'd needed this. I needed her so impossibly close that I didn't know where she ended and I began. I needed to feel her breath on my cheek as our lips grazed and hear the sounds she made when my teeth bit her bottom lip.

If I were murdered later for it, then I would die a happy man.

Our kisses grew messy as my hands finally touched every part of her I'd kept myself away from. Her side and her hip, and then her thigh and her ample backside. She was perfect in my arms—just like I'd dreamed of.

Stella broke the kiss, chest heaving. She gulped in a couple of deep breaths before saying, "I've waited long enough. Touch me, Alden."

"Is this what you want?"

"Of course it is. Trust me, you'll feel it."

I wanted this. I wanted *her*, and I couldn't deny it anymore. My hand gripped her hip, but I slowly moved it down to slip past the waistband of her leggings. When my fingers found her slick folds, I groaned.

"Fuck."

"I told you," she said. "Now make me come, Alden Canes. I know you can."

I moved my hand up and down, caressing her sensitive bud. She gasped and her jaw dropped open. I couldn't resist a smile. If I did my job right, there would be no more words out of her.

Stella's body arched into mine, and my lips returned to hers as I stroked her. I didn't think she could get more wet, yet as her pleasure grew, so did her slickness.

"O-oh, *shit*," she said, pulling her lips away from mine. "I-I'm gonna—"

I kept up the pace, torturing her with every centimeter I moved. Her mouth dropped open into a silent scream. I watched every second, content to sear it into my memory just like I had the first time I'd been with her.

Her chest heaved as she came on my hand.

"Want more?" My voice was low and gravelly under the weight of my desire.

"You remembered?"

"Of fucking course I did. Now how do you want to come again?"

"On your cock," she gasped. I opened my mouth to ask if she was sure, but her hands moved to my shoulders. "I'm taking over."

She hauled herself on top of me after pulling off my jeans and her leggings. My cock was pressed against her inner thigh, and I saw stars at the mere idea of entering her.

But I caught her by the hips.

"Stella," I said. "Slow down. We have all the time in the world."

She blinked. "I don't want you to change your mind."

"I won't." I hadn't for seven years.

"But—"

"Stella, you have to trust me. I know it's hard after—"

"I do trust you."

I didn't deserve it, but I would take it and never break it again.

"Then you have to believe me when I say there's no

rush. Let's enjoy this." I leaned up, pressing my palm under her sweater and moving up until I grazed her mid-back. "No bra?"

"A bra is a menace." She shrugged and my eyes caught on the outline of her breasts. I could see her nipples hardening through her sweater and it reminded me of the task at hand.

I kept going up until my hand had her neck. I pressed a rough kiss to the sensitive skin there, getting rewarded by a broken gasp from her. Then I moved to pull the sweater off of her body.

And God. She was incredible.

"Take your shirt off," she said. "I didn't get to see that the last time we did this, and I won't miss out again."

"Yes, ma'am."

I did as I was told, and then she lined me up with her core.

"Wait, do we need a condom?"

"I'm on birth control," she said. "And I've been tested two months ago. And I haven't had . . ." She bit her lip. "I've been with no one else since those tests."

"Reed didn't fuck you?"

"He was usually tired from his workouts."

"He's an idiot," I said. "He could have had you and he was too focused on himself." The head of my cock caught against her entrance. "I've been tested too," I said. "So let me show you exactly how you should feel."

"P-please."

I never thought we would be here again, not in real life, yet it seemed the impossible had happened.

Slowly, inch by inch, she sank down. I saw stars and tried my best not to surge forward and push all the way in. I'd been waiting for this day for far too long, but I wouldn't blow it by coming too fast.

Once I was seated all the way in, I could feel every flutter of Stella's pussy. I bit my tongue, trying not to lose control. Then, I caught sight of the goddess above me.

Stella's eyes were shut, her head tilted back. I had a perfect view of her breasts, her hips.

Every single inch of her.

"What else do you need?" I asked.

"Touch my clit again and let me ride you."

I loved the way she told me what to do. I loved the way she knew exactly what she wanted.

And I loved giving her what she wanted.

Stella moved her hips as I moved my thumb on her sensitive bud. She let out a gasp and jerked harder and she clenched on me as she moved.

I bit my lip to prevent myself from coming right then and there. The sight of her incredible body on mine, the way her tits moved as she found the pleasure she needed, the comfortable weight of her on my lap, and her hair falling over her shoulder was almost too much.

She found a rhythm, and I could see her losing herself in the feeling. Her jaw was open, and she moved jerkily. I watched every second of it as she came a second time.

"That was . . ." She trailed off. "God, I want to make you feel just as good. Let me get off you—"

"No," I nearly growled. "You stay right there."

"You can't be comfortable."

"Oh, I am *very* comfortable." It was my turn to move, and I thrust into her, reaching new depths. Her jaw dropped, and I gripped her hips before I picked up speed. She bounced with every movement, her breasts other-worldly in front of me. Her mouth formed an O, and her hand snaked its way down to her clit.

"God," she gasped the second she touched herself.

"That's right. Come on my cock a second time."

I was *so* close, but I bit the side of my cheeks to hold off.

"*Fuck.*" Her hips moved in time with mine. Her body jerked again and she clenched around me once more, her walls tight on my desperate cock.

And that's when I fell apart. My orgasm exploded through me, giving me the hottest burst of pleasure I'd ever experienced in my life.

When I came to my senses, Stella was panting above me.

"Are you human?" she asked.

"I am. Why?"

"Sex shouldn't feel that good."

It only did with her. I'd known that for years.

"It can when you find the right person."

She leaned down, crossing her arms over my chest

with a smirk on her face. "So I was right about the whole feelings thing."

"That is *not* what you should get from that."

"Definitely not, but you can't say I'm wrong when you're still inside of me."

I huffed out a laugh and leaned my head back. "Fine. I'll keep my mouth shut for once."

She rolled her eyes and pressed one kiss to my lips before slowly getting off of me and heading for the bathroom.

I waited for the familiar anxiety to seep in. I knew I was wrong. I knew I was going to be in so much trouble for this.

But when Stella came back out dressed in nothing, all thoughts vanished in a puff of smoke.

"Thanks to you, I feel like I can sleep for a week."

I laughed. "I could too."

She bit her lip. "Want to share heat again? I think I'll need it."

"And clothing?"

"Optional."

She was going to kill me. I knew she was.

"Then the answer is very much yes."

FIFTEEN

CONSCIOUSNESS CAME BACK SLOWLY. My body carried the memories of what Alden and I had done last night, and I felt satiated in a way I never had before.

For a second, I basked in the feeling of it. He was lying behind me, a thick arm slung over my waist. It was perfect.

But then the thoughts snuck in.

The last time we'd had sex didn't end well. Would he change his mind again, or would I be enough this time?

As much as I liked to think I could banish all of my self-doubt into the pits of hell, I couldn't. They stuck around, fed by every single person who'd hurt me.

Alden always held a piece of me, whether it be a childhood crush or this dangerous feeling that could turn all-encompassing at any time. I was careening toward a train wreck of my own making. And I couldn't even tell Winnie what I was doing.

I missed the world, yet the quiet of the storm, with no one else talking in my ear and telling me who or what I should be, also led to all of my worries creeping in.

"Are you awake this time?" he asked me, pulling me out of my thoughts.

"Learned your lesson, huh?"

"Not spilling any more secrets."

I let out a soft laugh and sat up. I winced when I realized how sticky I was. "God, I miss hot water heaters."

"Do you?" he asked with a smile. "Have I ever told you how lucky you are that Amma has old shit?"

"No, why?"

"I lit the pilot last night on the water heater."

"I have no idea what that means."

"It means you have hot water. No electricity needed. Most models can't be lit, but hers was visible, and it primarily runs off of gas, so it worked."

For a second, I couldn't comprehend what he was saying. I was laying here afraid that he'd take it all back. Instead, he was solving problems I didn't know had solutions.

"You lit a gas machine on fire so I could have hot water? Isn't that dangerous?"

"Not that dangerous, but it is if you don't know what you're doing."

Still. I didn't expect him to think twice about it. My cheeks erupted in heat, adding to the feelings that swirled within me for him.

Goddammit. I needed him to stop being so *perfect*. If he didn't, then I'd want this forever.

"Best Christmas present ever," I managed to say. "Thank you."

"I'm not letting you get that cold again," he said. His lips pressed against my cheek.

With him kissing me, I had all the warmth I needed.

"Yeah, I'll definitely need a shower if we're repeating last night. We *are* repeating it, right?"

"Of course. Not exactly like that, but we'll do the act again."

"What, you don't like doing the same thing over and over?"

"With a woman like you? Absolutely not."

My mind flashed to all the things we could do, including in the very place I was going.

"Want to join me?" I asked.

"In the shower?"

"No," I said, rolling my eyes, "in the snow."

"You're hilarious." He kissed my neck. "But can you continue to be while I distract you?"

"First, I need a shower," I said. "That's not negotiable."

"Then I'll join you."

I got up, but then his hand smacked my ass and I yelped. "What the—"

"Sorry, couldn't resist. It's too perfect."

"I'm pretty sure my ass is not perfect."

He raised an eyebrow, daring me to continue.

Now my face was on fire. "Okay, I'll shut up."

"Good. No more putting yourself down. Talk about yourself as I see you."

"And how do you see me?"

"As the perfection you are."

I could only stare at him, trying to find a lie that wasn't there. Eventually, it was too much, and I darted into the shower.

A few moments later, Alden followed. By that time, the water was steaming, creating an oasis of warmth inside the icy house.

I moaned when I stepped in.

"I think you're the perfect one," I said as the heated water cascaded down my back. "Just for this water alone. It's truly spectacular."

"It's nothing compared to my view."

Goddammit. Could I even handle the full wattage of his compliments? I didn't think it was possible.

"You know, I owe you one for this shower."

"Owe me one of what?"

"Get in here and find out."

Alden didn't waste any time as he stepped into the warm spray of the water. I took in his chest and body for one second before I sunk to my knees.

"What are you doing?"

"Giving you a gift." I looked up at him, ignoring the water around me.

"I didn't do this to get anything in return."

"But you'll enjoy this, right?"

Alden's hand cupped my cheek, stopping me as I moved to take him into my mouth.

"Stella, I need you to know that I did this because I wanted you to have something you enjoy. I'll *always* do nice things for you, and you never have to repay that."

His words were too soft and too kind. "I understand. Thank you." But then I smiled. "I still want to suck your cock, though."

"Jesus Christ," he said. "Nothing stops you, huh?"

"Nope. Now shut the fuck up."

Alden was already half hard, but he thickened in my mouth the second it closed around him. He muttered a soft curse as I sucked. His hands went through my hair, pulling me in closer. I let his hardness surge deep in my mouth before I pulled out and did it over again.

I worshiped his cock, running my tongue over every millimeter of it, enjoying each one of his moans.

"Stella, you're killing me here."

"What do you want?" My hand jerked him off while I spoke. "Do you want to come?"

"Yes."

"Then fuck my mouth like you mean it." My mouth went back to its work, and his hips jerked into me. I let him lose control, using my hand to grip him all the way to the hilt.

"Stella, you're so fucking hot when you're sucking me off."

God, I was going to have to be in here for years to work out the tension between my legs.

His thrusts became erratic, and I tasted the salt as he came in my mouth. I took my time to savor every last drop and wiped my lip when I was done.

"Good?"

"Jesus Christ," he said. "Get up here."

Alden pulled me to my feet and captured my mouth with his. This kiss was hot and messy, and we were both soaked under the spray of the shower.

"I guess that's a yes."

"I'm going to make you forget how to be a smart-ass," he muttered.

"Joke's on you, I'm always a—" Words fell away when he brought me close and pressed two fingers into my core.

"Whatever you're saying, Stella, save it for later."

His thumb pressed against my clit and I gasped. It was his turn to torture me. His movements were slow and controlled, but they sent my already revved-up body into a higher gear. I could feel pleasure all throughout me as I built to something impossibly greater.

Alden's fingers hooked, hitting my G-spot with enough force to make me see stars. I let out a moan, rutting against his hand to get the release I needed.

"F-fuck." I finally came. Pleasure shot through every one of the cells in my body. I didn't see stars; I saw the universe.

Alden's mouth went to my neck as I came down from my high. "What were you going to say?"

"I don't fucking remember," I said. "Just kiss me."

His lips met mine, and I lost myself in him as we made out under the spray of the water. A few minutes later, my body was begging for more.

"I regret giving you that blowjob right now."

"Why?"

"Because I'd love for you to fuck me."

Alden huffed out a laugh. "Do you think so lowly of me?" He pressed his erection into my leg. "I'll fuck you any time you want."

"How the *hell*—"

"I've been saving this up for a long time, baby." His voice was rough and close to my ear. "I can go as long as you want."

"Yes," I gasped out. I found the strength to turn. "Please."

He wasted no time in lining himself up with me. Once he'd found his mark, he impaled me with one ruthless thrust.

I could only gasp at the invasion. The water was getting cold, but I didn't care because this felt so *right*.

While he was buried to the hilt, I had one second to suck in a breath before he pounded into me again, sending me into the wall as he let loose.

"Oh *god*."

"Touch yourself," he said. "Come again."

I didn't need to be told twice. His movements burned in the perfect way—the one that made orgasms far easier. I was halfway there by the time my hand found my clit, and it didn't take long for me to build up again.

My moans changed when I got close, and his hand snaked to my breast, pinching my nipple as his own thrusts grew erratic.

When he came in me, I did the same on him. I lost sight as I felt the eruption of perfect heat throughout my body. The universe danced behind my eyelids again, brought forth by the man who knew me better than anyone else.

"You're too good at this," I managed to say.

"Water's cold," he said as his lips pressed into my shoulder.

"I don't care."

"You will. Let me keep you warm."

How could I say no to that?

We finished up quickly, and just as he turned off the water, the coolness seeped in.

After we dressed, we huddled in front of the fire. It was Christmas morning, and I should have been sad, but in the silence of the living room, with the fire going and the snow lying on the ground outside, it felt so cozy. Alden was stoking the fire, a flannel over his shoulders.

This was picturesque, and I knew I needed to remember this moment. I grabbed the Polaroid and held it up.

"Alden," I called. He turned with a smile and I snapped the picture.

"What was that for?"

"It's a good moment," I said. "I like to remember those."

It printed, and I waited for it to develop. When it was done, I took a glance, only for my breath to be stolen.

I'd seen Alden at his worst and at what I thought was his best. At every given moment, he had a sadness simmering under the surface of every smile he gave, and I always wished it wasn't there.

But this time, I only saw joy. His eyes crinkled when he was happy and the shadow of his beard did nothing to hide the full stretch of his lips into a grin.

I'd *never* seen this before.

My breath caught in my throat.

"Don't tell me I was making a weird face," he said.

"N-no. You look great."

My heart was in a dangerous place, teetering on feelings that would break me if this ended the same way it had seven years ago.

I didn't think I could come back from that kind of heartbreak.

"What's wrong?" he asked. All traces of that perfect smile were gone from his face.

He was *concerned*, just like he had been when he saw how sad I was.

I sifted through my memories of us. He'd always been this way. He saw when I was sad and celebrated when I was happy. We had a real chance at working, and to this day, I didn't know what went wrong and why he turned me down.

I always thought it was me, or that he just didn't see

me that way, but the last day proved to me that he felt *something*, even if he was in denial about it.

"Stella," he urged. "What's going through your head?"

How did I ask him what the hell was going on when he seemed hell-bent on not talking about it? How did I tell him I was falling for him with the risk of getting heartbroken again?

I had no idea what to do.

But I didn't get a chance to answer.

The lights flashed, electricity running through the house for all of a second before it flickered out again. Both of us looked up, bewildered. It flickered on again and stayed.

"Power," I said. "We finally have power."

The words felt wrong as they left my mouth. While we had electricity again, I realized that *I* didn't have any power at all.

Because I had no idea how this would end.

SIXTEEN

THE HOUSE TRANSFORMED with the return of electricity.
All of the lights flickered to life, and Amma's ceiling fan
rotated in the corner, moving the stale air.

But Stella had barely moved. She still had that down-
trodden expression on her face, one that I needed to
know the reason for.

"So what were you saying?" I asked, closing up the
stove.

"I . . . We should check up on everyone." She got up
without another word and went for the phone.

Shit. She was upset—I could hear it in her voice. What
the fuck had I done? The sex had been good and she was
fine until we came out here. I looked around the room to
see if there was something that could have caused it, but
it was the same living room we'd spent the last few
days in.

The photo she'd taken of me sat innocently on the

couch, but it only showed me smiling. I got up slowly, still lost.

I found her beside the phone, shuffling through Amma's address book.

"Hank . . . Hank . . . Got it! Found her neighbor's number."

She dialed, still not looking at me. I moved close to listen.

"Hello? Stella, is that you?"

My chest loosened when we heard Amma's voice.

"Yes, Amma," she said. "Are you okay?"

"Oh, honey, we're fine. Hank has a power generator, so I've been living a life of luxury. I barely missed anything."

"Good," Stella said. "I hated not being able to see you."

"How are you, dear? Is anyone dead?"

"No. We had a couple of close calls, but we're good."

"And the stove worked for both of you?"

"Yes, it kept us warm. I'm glad you didn't get rid of it."

"And I'm glad you had Alden. Is he nearby?"

"I'm here, Amma," I said.

"Good! I hope Stella wasn't too hard on you."

"It was nothing I didn't deserve."

Stella's eyes flickered to me for one second before turning back to the wall.

"Is Hank's house closer to the road? Can you see if they're cleared?"

"It's a little closer. I saw the electric company when

they came by. They had those chains on their trucks, and they were still sliding. I think it's good to stay put."

Stella was probably disappointed, but I wasn't. More time where I could be with her before all of this blew up? I'd take it.

I would have more time to figure out what had upset her too.

"Okay," Stella said. "If you need me—"

"I'm fine. I'm more worried about *you*. Do you have enough food still?"

"We have more than enough."

"And I've kept the fire going," I added. "Having the heat back will help."

"Good. Stay put and stay safe."

"I will."

"I'm so glad to hear from you. And give your brother a call. He wants an update."

Shit.

Nick.

I hadn't thought of him since being with Stella again, and the guilt hit me like a pile of bricks. Would she tell him immediately? Would everything fall apart right in front of her?

What was worse, I wasn't so sure I could break it off, not when I'd found myself so intrinsically bound to her.

"Did the city fare better than we did?" she asked.

"Somewhat. This is still a storm for the storybooks, but they have snowplows that we don't. Nick didn't realize how nerve-racking it would be. He's been calling here every day, making sure we still see the smoke from the chimney."

"Can you even see your house from there?"

"Not really, but Hank walked outside. It made Nick feel better."

"I'll call now. Thanks, Amma."

"Give me a shout if you need anything. And Merry Christmas!"

Stella's face fell. "Yeah, you too. It doesn't feel the same."

"We'll have an extra-special party to make up for it. Don't you worry."

She nodded and said her goodbyes. Stella didn't look at me while she called Nick. I was glad she didn't glance over because then she'd see the panic on my face.

He answered on the first ring. "Stella? Please tell me you're okay."

"I'm fine. Well, as fine as I can be considering the fact that I *just* got hot water back. Amma's stove came in handy, though."

"How's Alden? Is he okay?"

"He's right next to me. Say hi." She leaned the phone over, and I swallowed.

"H-hey."

She did a double take, immediately picking up on my discomfort. There would be questions after this call, and I needed to decide how to explain what Nick and I had discussed seven years ago.

But then all thoughts flew out the window when Nick said his next sentence.

"You held up on your deal, right? You took care of her?"

Stella blinked, brows pulling low on her forehead. That . . . didn't sound the best, I'd admit.

"Take care of me?" she repeated.

"Well, yeah." Nick said it like it was obvious. "I figured it would be easier if I tried to get him to talk to you. From what I've heard, Winnie did too."

Stella slowly looked over at me, eyes narrowed. "So not only do I need to be taken care of, but if it weren't for you two, I'd have been spending the last few days in silence?"

"Well maybe—"

"How about we stay glad that everyone is okay?" I asked. "It's all fine."

Stella's glare told me everything was *not* fine.

"Look at you communicating. I'm glad I called you and that she was receptive to it. I know how stubborn both of you are."

Stella's lips pressed together, and now she looked one second away from killing *both* of us.

"Yeah."

"And no . . . other issues?"

Issues. I knew what he was referring to, but it was easier to pretend he was talking about us fighting.

"No."

"Cool, cool. Let me know if anything goes down. And

Stella, it's melting out here, so I'll get your stuff from Reed's soon."

"Thank you," she said, but her voice was still colder than the ice outside.

"I need to get going. The office made us all work from home, so I'm technically supposed to be in a meeting. But I'm *so* glad you're safe."

He hung up and Stella wasted no time whirling on me.

"What the *fuck*?"

"That sounded worse than it is."

"Yeah, it does. How about we skip the guessing and you explain it to me, then?"

"I would have taken care of you either way."

"Are you sure? Because you certainly had no problem staying away before both he and Winnie called you. The timing is suspicious."

"The timing means nothing."

"Then explain yourself. You can't just ignore me for seven years and then expect me to accept this new side of you out of nowhere."

"I can't . . . Let's not—"

"No, we need to talk about this, especially if we're in a relationship."

"Maybe we shouldn't . . ." I paused. The words couldn't come out. Not even thinking of the words Nick said to me could make me say that we shouldn't be together.

"Are you about to tell me we can't be together?" She

crossed her arms over her chest. "Because this time, I'll need a good fucking reason for that."

The right answer was to say yes. I could make up some stupid excuse and walk away. We could never mention this again, and Nick would remain my friend.

But I fucking couldn't.

I should have never been with her again because the idea of leaving hurt more now than it ever did all that time ago.

I slumped forward, my hand meeting my forehead. I didn't know what to say or what was right. For years, I got by with thinking I was keeping my friendship.

But now I didn't know if it was worth it.

"I *can't* say it, Stella. I can't let you down. Not again. Just like I couldn't leave you here. I will *always* take care of you."

"Then why did you break my heart the first time? In a *text* of all things?"

"I couldn't be with you."

Her jaw dropped for all of one second, but then she exploded. "Why, Alden? Why do this? Is there some cosmic force telling you not to be around me or something?"

And there it was. The question I didn't know how to answer.

"It's complicated."

"Why is it complicated?"

I opened my mouth to give her another diversion, but

there weren't any I could give. I couldn't lie to her, and I couldn't hide to make this go away.

I should choose Nick. He was my best friend and he asked me not to do this with his sister. But I couldn't continue being a coward. I couldn't continue justifying breaking her heart to keep him comfortable.

"Because Nick told me not to date you seven years ago."

Silence stretched out like a highway between us.

Finally, she spoke. "He *what?*"

"He's trying to protect you."

She shook her head, jaw still hanging open. "From who? *You?* You're not a threat."

"Am I not? I'm a guy going after his sister. He's bound to feel weird about it."

"If we live in the eighteen hundreds, maybe. Last I checked it's the twenty-first century."

"I slept with you when you were eighteen."

"And?"

"That's predatory."

"Pred—*what?* I came onto *you.* I was an adult!"

"And I was *more* of an adult. Four years older than you."

"You're not making any sense. Even if you're right, the only person who gets to have a say in who I date is *me* and the person I choose to be with. No one else."

"He cares about you."

"Then he should trust me, and you for that matter.

You're his best friend, and last I checked, it comes with some amount of trust."

"Trust that I broke."

"Tell me how, Alden. Just by sleeping with me?"

"Yes."

She scoffed. "Did you force me into it?"

"No."

"Were you in a position of power over me?"

"*No.*"

"Then explain it to me like I'm five. Because I don't get it. And leave out any misguided notions that my brother needs to protect me. I can take care of myself, thank you very much."

I didn't have an answer for it. Over the years, I never questioned Nick's reasoning for wanting me away from his sister.

But in the face of Stella, I was starting to.

"That's what I thought," she said. "God, I can't believe him. I can't believe *you* let him talk to you like that."

"He had good points."

"Oh, what were they? That I'm too fragile or delicate?"

"That the justifications I used to sleep with you were the same ones my dad used when talking about his new wife."

She blinked, obviously not expecting that answer. "Wh-what?"

"You're the same age as her, you know. And I knew it was different. I'm his son, and I'm nowhere near his age.

But I told Nick you were an adult. That you consented, and you were fine with it. Then he said I sounded a lot like my dad. And he was right. I did."

"You don't honestly believe that, do you?"

"It's not exactly the same, but you were off-limits, and I broke his trust. Nick made it clear. If I went after you, he and I wouldn't be friends."

"He threatened to drop you?"

"Yes."

"No fucking way. Why would he—you're his *best friend*."

"Which makes it worse that I went after you."

"We were friends too!" she said. "I don't . . . Why would he get in the middle of something like that? Why would he threaten you? This isn't okay."

"It's not . . . He wasn't—"

"And *you*! You didn't call him out or find *anything* wrong with that? You just did what he said, no questions asked?"

"I thought it was the right thing. He told me to choose between you or him and—"

Stella huffed out a humorless laugh. "You chose him."

"I—" I couldn't say anything else. The words killed me. She was right. In the end, I chose my friend over her.

I knew what it was like not to be chosen. It had happened too many times in my life, and as I saw my own pain echoing in her, I regretted my choice more than I thought possible.

I deserved for her to hate me. It would kill me to see

it, especially after we'd gotten along over the last few days, but it was what I deserved.

"I'm sorry, Stella."

She shook her head, her anger dissipating. "I don't want to hear sorry right now. I'm gonna go back in the bedroom."

"It's freezing in there."

"The heat is on. I need a minute to think."

"I'll go outside."

"Stop it. I don't want you going out there to suffer because you think you have to. Just give me a minute." She gathered a blanket and went to the back room, slamming the door behind her.

I had to fight every muscle in my body not to chase her down.

But she was right. I didn't choose her. I chose a friendship I cherished.

And hurt her in the process.

SEVENTEEN

RULE NUMBER one when running to a room to stew in feelings: bring your phone.

I failed rule number one.

Since the power was back on, I wanted to talk to Winnie. Her advice would more than likely be to send Alden and Nick down a cliff with no brakes, but hearing her voice would help.

But my phone was still powered off in the living room and all I had were my thoughts.

My mind oscillated from understanding why Alden did what he did to being furious that he didn't choose me.

On the one hand, I knew that if I were in the same position with Winnie, I would have picked her.

On the other hand, Winnie never would have fucking asked me to choose in the first place.

My conflicting feelings, mixed with my own self-doubts, added to my terrible mood. What if I'd been different—would he have chosen me? What could I have done to make him want me?

Could I have been a different person?

That was the worst part of it all. My doubts were far worse now.

I wanted him to want me. All of me.

But he chose someone else.

I laid in Amma's bed for who knows how long, going over everything I'd learned with a fine-tooth comb. I didn't know what to feel, only that I wasn't happy with how things turned out.

I didn't realize that I'd fallen asleep until my eyes shot open and it was night outside. Hours had passed, and I didn't feel any better about what had happened.

For a while, I sat in the darkness, wishing I could go back to sleep and forget it all for a little longer. But then, a knock at the door interrupted my train of thought.

"What?" I asked. "I don't want to talk if that's what you're about to ask."

"Okay," he replied. "But I made you food."

That got my attention. After stewing all day, I needed something in my stomach. My mind was on all the delicious things he could have made, but when I cracked the door, I only saw soup.

"Seriously?"

"Sorry, it's all we have."

"I'll make it work," I said as I grabbed the bowl and shut the door.

I heard him sigh on the other side of it.

"You can't be mad that I want to be alone," I told him.

"I'm not mad at you."

"You're not happy about something."

"I'm mad that I made the choice I did, but not at you for reacting to it."

I stared at the soup bowl for a second. "Thanks. Now let's go back to not talking."

"I'll give you your space in a minute. I can't let you sit in there any longer without you knowing one thing."

"If it's that you're sorry, I'm not ready to hear that again."

"No, it's not that. Just listen for a second, Stella. Just for a second."

"Fine."

I heard him take a shaky breath. "I know you're in there thinking that this is somehow your fault, and it's not. It's mine. I made the wrong choice, Stella. I know that now. Nick said things about me that I feared were true, and I let myself walk away from you and break your heart. But I never should have. I regretted it even then. I counted the *days* that we were apart, suffering through each one of them like a fucking idiot when you were right there."

Tears gathered in my eyes. "Y-you counted the days?"

"All 2,561 of them. At first, I didn't know why I was doing it, but then it continued. No woman could hold a candle to you. I love your laugh, your sarcasm, and your hardheadedness. And because of my stupid choice, you spent those years questioning everything about yourself. You're not a problem, Stella. You're the solution. You're everything, and I fucked it up. I know it. I should have chosen you all of those years ago because now I know that it'll always be *you*. And yeah, it may ruin things with Nick. And maybe I won't even have you in the end because you could find someone else. But I'll be here, always here. I'm yours. Forever yours."

Footsteps walked away, leaving me with the sound of my pounding heart. I put the soup on the side table, completely uninterested in eating, and ran for the man who told me everything I needed to hear.

I'd never heard him sound like that, not to anyone. I didn't think I was important to him.

But obviously, I was wrong.

"You can't just say shit like that and walk away!" I snapped at the sight of his shoulders.

He turned. "You said you needed space."

"But then you told me you counted the *days* we were apart. That changes everything."

"Does it?" he asked slowly. "Because the way I see it—"

"Nope, you're done talking. It's my turn now." His eyes widened, but he didn't say anything else. "Thank you. Now, first of all, fuck you for not choosing me. I'm great, and I deserve someone who sees it."

"You do." His voice was soft. "You deserve that and more."

"And that leads me to my next point." I sucked in a

lungful of air before continuing. "Thank you for being the only one who actually saw it."

He blinked, obviously not expecting my second point. "What?"

"You reminded me that I'm worth something again. You've treated me like no other partner in my life has."

"Guys should have lined up for you, Stella. You should have never felt like you did."

"And I won't again. This time, if I go all in with someone, it'll be with someone who's promised to choose me. Someone who'll treat me as I should be."

"That's exactly what you should do. I know I'll never be him—"

"That's the thing, though," I said. "You could be—if you tried."

"I don't think I deserve—"

"Stop saying you don't deserve it. You're the man who ran in the snow to be sure I wasn't alone through this. You kept a fire going, relit the pilot light on the water heater, and stayed with me through thick and thin during this snowstorm. You're a good person, Alden. Fuck anyone who says anything differently."

He blinked as if he'd never heard that before. "But I hurt you."

"Yeah, and it was over two thousand days ago." I poked his chest. "I think you've made up for it. So, let's try it again this time. And not let anyone else tell us what to do."

His hand covered mine. "Are you sure?"

"Are *you* sure you can handle me?"

"Very sure. I've wanted to since that night at the Christmas party."

With a smile, I pulled away from his grip and cupped his face before pulling him into a searing kiss.

Everything was right in the world.

I had Alden and I finally knew everything.

"Wait," he said, pulling away far too soon. "We still need to talk about everything that happened."

"We do. But I couldn't let you walk away without you knowing I feel the same way."

"You do?"

"I always have. I've had a crush on you since I was a kid. I thought I wasn't good enough for you."

"You're more than good enough for me."

"I finally believe it," I said.

His eyes fell to my lips, and I thought he would kiss me again, but he pulled away.

"Where are you going?"

"To make you something. We'll need a drink if we're about to rehash everything we just opened up."

EIGHTEEN

"So, what kind of drink are you making?" Stella followed me to the kitchen. "Amma only has moonshine, and I doubt she'd want to share. Or that I'd even want that paint thinner in my body."

"I don't know how she drinks that stuff." I shook my head. "And no, I didn't mean *that* kind of drink. What are the odds that Amma has evaporated milk?"

"For what?"

"Hot chocolate. I have a recipe."

"And it uses evaporated milk?"

"No, but I can make it work. Whatever actual milk was here went bad a few days ago."

She walked to the cabinet with the food, pulling out a can. "High, I guess. Thank God for her always over-buying at the store."

I took the can and grabbed a pot.

"I thought you didn't cook."

"I don't, but whenever I would think too hard about the past, I would experiment with hot chocolate."

"Why?"

"It's your favorite. It made me feel connected to you."

Her lips went slack before curving into a full smile. "That's really sweet, actually."

"Not with the context, but I'm happy it's coming in handy now." I stirred the pot and waited for the milk to warm. I added cocoa powder and sugar before tasting it myself to be sure it was close to what I usually made. "It's not perfect."

"Oh, come on. I still want it. This can't be worse than Reed's."

I laughed. "If it is, you have permission to dump me."

She took the mug with a smile. "I'll deal with bad hot chocolate for you." She lifted it and took a sip, and her eyes went wide.

"What's the verdict?"

"Holy *shit*," she said. "This is the best I've ever had."

"Is it? It's better with regular milk."

"I'm coming off from two years of nearly no sugar and powdered hot chocolate." She shrugged before her smile returned. "Seems like you're the best I've had in multiple ways."

"You're shameless."

"And you're blushing."

I rubbed my warm cheek. "Before we get too off track, we should finish our conversation."

She blew out a breath. "I know. I'm just stalling a

little." She took another long drink before gesturing to the living room.

I took a second to put the bed back into the couch so we could sit comfortably.

Stella wasted no time once she sat. "Nick shouldn't have done what he did. I stand by it, but I don't get why you went along with it for so long."

"Sometimes friendship means suffering."

She blinked and shook her head. "What? No, it doesn't."

"We all have to sacrifice things to be around others. Hasn't there been something Winnie has asked of you that hurts?"

"No. Winnie knows I'm my own person. Even when I was being an idiot with Reed, she told me her opinions, but she never forced my hand like Nick did yours. The only time that could be justified is if there was some sort of abuse involved, but that's not what happened with you and me."

"There's really nothing?"

"No. Why do you think that it's okay for friends to dictate how we live our lives?"

"I either be what they want, or they leave." I shrugged, trying to ignore the pain in my chest as I thought about my past. "It's life for me."

"First of all, anyone who leaves you has something wrong with *them*. It's never your fault. And second of all, we choose our friends. If they hurt you, then something is wrong."

"But I owe Nick for saving my ass as a kid."

"Friendships don't come with IOUs, not healthy ones, at least."

"So, you don't feel like you owe Winnie for anything?"

"No. I'm grateful for a lot of the things she's done, but at the end of the day, I just like being around her."

"I can't imagine a friendship like that. There's no disagreements?"

"There are, but there's never a thing that we've been unable to figure out. Love doesn't have to hurt."

"I don't think I know how to love someone without hurting."

"Okay, what about this, then? Us? Does it hurt?"

"The guilt does."

"Take that out since we're working on it right now. Have *I*, not Nick, asked you to do anything that hurts?"

"No."

"There's one example right there, then."

"I want to believe you, it's just . . . this has been my life for too long. Nothing comes without a cost."

"That's because I haven't been around. I'll change it."

"Nick is going to be mad."

"And?"

"I've *never* seen him like that, Stella. At least not with me. I'm sure you've fought, but this was another level. It's not the man you know."

She pressed her lips together. "He could have matured."

"And if he didn't?"

"Then I'm seeing my brother for the man that he is. We all see people's true colors eventually."

"I don't want you to fight with your brother for me."

"And I didn't want him to fight with *you* for me. Don't you see the common denominator? He was unreasonable then. And if he is now, then whatever happens is on him."

I huffed out a laugh. "You'll really stand up to him?"

"He deserves it for what he did seven years ago."

Stella made all of my worries sound so manageable. I'd never been around anyone who could do that. "I should have told you what he did."

"I'm guessing you were afraid of the consequences if you did."

"Very." I rubbed the back of my neck. "I still am. But . . . I'm sorry it took seven years for us to talk about it."

"I was mad. You were living in fear. It doesn't help that we're both stubborn. We just had to wait for a snowstorm to give us a second chance."

"I still can't believe you're even giving me one."

"I can. Remember my high school crush? No one wanted me anyway, but I wanted you."

I winced. "That's not . . . entirely true."

"*What?*"

"We caught a couple of guys talking about you once. One wanted to ask you out and see how quickly you'd sleep with him."

Stella's face twisted. "Really? Like some sort of bet to see if the ugly girl would put out?"

"Stella, you were beautiful, even if some people didn't

see it. You were nice to everyone, always smiling. Other than that fucker, you had options, but you were around us all the time."

"Well, shitty guys have always been a part of my life, so that trend probably would have continued."

"I'm not going to be one of them."

Her smile was soft, and no cell in my body could find a way to regret this choice.

I was able to sneak in one kiss before the home phone rang again, which pulled Stella away. It was her parents checking in, eager to hear that we were both okay after being secluded for so long. Stella and I told them about our adventures and then grabbed another muffin for a snack.

"Is that blueberry?"

"Unfortunately, I'm tired of the chocolate ones." She took a bite and then grimaced. "Correction: I'm tired of *all* of them. Even the soup."

"I hope all soup isn't off the menu," I replied. "Because the first thing I'm asking for is that chicken and gnocchi soup."

She laughed. "I don't know how you can even think about soup after we've only eaten that and muffins."

"Then we can have something else—as long as you made it. I'll eat your cooking every damn day if I can, Stella."

"I'm still out of practice. What if I burn things?"

"Then I'll eat that too."

NINETEEN

THE NEXT MORNING, I woke up and quickly realized how every inch of me was wrapped around Alden. I grimaced, remembering when Reed would say I was cutting off his circulation and tried to pull away.

"Where do you think you're going?" He pulled me in tighter.

"I'm suffocating you."

"You're absolutely not. Stay in my arms, Stella. It's right where I want you."

Cheeks heating, I did as I was told.

I didn't want to move anyway. Alden was more comfortable than the most expensive pillow I owned. The fact that he wanted me as close as I wanted him sent butterflies into my stomach.

All I could do was nuzzle my face into his neck and let his beard tickle my cheek.

I was gone. *So* gone. Nothing would compare to this.

Alden's hand traced lazy circles on my back, and I lost myself to the quiet peace of the moment. I don't know how long we sat there simply enjoying each other's company.

"I can't believe Christmas is over," I eventually said.

"I think it's extended for this year, especially since we spent most of the day without the Christmas tree even on."

I thought of the multicolored lights and the tacky decorations. They'd twinkled innocently in the corner of the living room, and Amma's icicle lights outside glowed in the snow now that the power was back on.

"Still," I said, sighing. "I spent the beginning of the season as someone else. I feel like I missed out on everything I loved. The tree, the music, the traditions."

"We have time now," he replied. "Come on."

I slowly stood, my body finally feeling rested after spending the night on a mattress and not a pullout couch. I followed Alden as he went to Amma's old record player, which was built into one of her tables. She had tons of classic Christmas vinyls, and in the rare times she hosted the holiday, they would be playing in the background.

The sound of an old record filled the space, mixed with crooning lyrics about the season.

"May I have this dance?" he asked.

I couldn't help but blush. "I haven't danced since high school."

"Yes, but you once mentioned you thought dancing to

Christmas music was one of the most romantic things you could imagine."

I swallowed. We'd been young when I'd said that. I still believed it, but as I got older, the idea seemed more and more like a childlike dream.

"I said that a long time ago."

"I always listened, Stella. Come on."

He spun me to the music, and a smile broke out on my face. I didn't know what it would feel like to finally get everything I wanted, but it was a warm glow, one that rivaled the tree.

I'd missed these records. I'd missed the fairy lights. I'd missed all of it over the two years I'd lost myself. And now I was whole again.

More than whole, because I had Alden with me.

And I didn't ever want him to leave.

We danced through the whole vinyl. It was nothing more than swaying to the music, but I loved every second of it.

I was leaning against his shoulder when I saw brightness through the closed curtain.

With the clouds, everything outside had been a mix of gray and white, but this was reflective in a way I hadn't seen in a while.

"Alden?" I asked. "What was the weather supposed to be like today?"

"No idea," he said, not sparing the window a second glance.

"Maybe we should check. It looks so bright, like . . ."

He finally turned. "The sun."

I nodded excitedly and opened the curtain. My eyes protested the assault of bright light, but it was clear that the sun was fully out, and the snow was receding, even if only slightly.

"Oh my God," I said with a gasp. "It's actually melting."

Alden checked his phone. "The temperature is above freezing."

"Do you know what this means?"

"Flooding."

I rolled my eyes. "No. Well, yes. But maybe we can get out of here."

"Huh. You might get to see your family on the day after Christmas after all."

I threw on my jacket and pulled him outside. There were still thick piles of snow, but it was slushy now. Out in the distance, I heard a car go by.

"Yes! People are out and about."

"We'll need to clear the driveway and call to see if the city is having the same luck."

"We can do all of those things." He grabbed my arm to stop me. "But first, breakfast."

I groaned. "Not another muffin."

"Hey, at least I can make more hot chocolate to wash it down."

Alden disappeared back into the house. I followed and grabbed another one of the cursed baked goods as Alden made more of my favorite drink.

"What's your first plan for when we get out of here?" he asked.

"Seeing what Nick got back from Reed. I miss having my own stuff."

The mention of Nick made Alden's lips press together. He was worried about telling him, and while I knew my brother was clearly in the wrong, I also knew how terrifying it had to be for Alden to be threatened by his best friend.

Even I couldn't imagine Nick and Alden not being friends—they'd always been a pair. I could only hope that Nick would see sense this time.

"You're not in this alone, remember?" I leaned over to touch his hand. "I'll tell him with you."

"He's my friend. I should tell him."

"He's *my* brother, and I reserve the right to tell him he's being an ass."

"It might not be pretty."

"If we really wanted it to get ugly, I could tell Winnie."

That finally got a smile out of Alden. "You think she would be on our side?"

"She's the one who told me to go after you at that party."

"Really? She didn't say anything about the age gap?"

"It's four years, not four decades. And we were on the same level intellectually at that point."

"Are you calling me dumb?"

"I'm calling *me* smart," I replied and squeezed his hand. "It's not gonna be a huge deal."

"I hope you're right."

"Enough about my dumbass brother. What are you going to do?"

"I need to be sure Ryan is okay at my house. I bet he had a frustrating week of people getting their asses injured."

"And I need to *see* the park," I said. "I can't believe I've never been."

"You'd like it. It's quiet, just like here."

"I need that," I said. "Will you show me around?"

"Of course I will."

I couldn't resist the smile on my face. This wasn't going to end just because we were free. The door was open for me to know every part of this man, and I wasn't going to deny myself that. I polished off my muffin in a few bites and stood. "All right. I've eaten. Let's go shovel."

"Are you excited to leave?"

"Yes," I nearly groaned. "I loved having time to ourselves, but I'd like to at least see *some* of my family for Christmas, or whatever we're calling the day after."

We walked into the cold and got the driveway shoveled. It was hard work since her driveway was so long, but the slush wasn't as stuck as it would have been if it were still below zero.

Once that was done, we walked to his truck, where we both tried to get all the snow off it. It took a long time to shove it out of every crevice, but eventually, it was cleared and we could get in.

I glanced at the back seat with a grin.

"What are you thinking about?" Alden asked.

"Oh, memories. Think we could still fit back there?"

"We could try," he said with a smile. "But first, let's see if I can get this thing out of this ditch."

We slid more than I had anticipated, but eventually, the truck pulled onto the road. Despite there being tire tracks, the few turns we took to get to Amma's were accompanied with terrifying slides, and I hoped we had an easy time getting out of here and into the city.

"We can't stay after it gets dark," he said. "All of this will be frozen over by then."

"Let's clean up a little and then find Amma. We should be able to make the walk to Hank's house."

We didn't waste time. He helped me clean up the mess we'd made. We folded blankets and took out the trash. When we were done, it was already the afternoon.

"Okay," I said, grabbing a jacket, "time to go find—"

I was interrupted by the front door opening. Amma's short form walked through. She was in a jacket too big for her, with snow-covered shoes.

Leave it to her to read my mind.

"Kids!" she called, eyes on her boots as she knocked the snow off on the entrance rug. "Are you decent?"

"Yes," I said, running to pull her into a tight hug. "God, it's so good to see you."

"You two as well. I'm *so* glad it finally warmed up. I missed my own house—not that Hank isn't great company."

"*Great* company?"

"Oh, don't you start. Your mom already asked me about my intentions with him." She rolled her eyes. "What did I do to make you guys ask so many questions?"

"You ask more questions than we ever could. It's payback, Amma."

"I'll let it slide, but only because you *finally* seem like yourself again. What has you in such a good mood?"

Alden and I hadn't talked about when we would tell others, but considering Nick's past issues with us, I could make an educated guess and say he should be the first to know. My family *loved* to talk, and if he found out from anyone but us, then it would make it worse.

"I needed to be here for a bit," I settled on. "I didn't realize how much I would enjoy being away from the city. Maybe I need more vacations."

"With electricity this time?" Alden added.

"What, are you tired from having to keep me alive?"

"More like tired of you feeling bad about letting me."

"Oh, shut up. You taught me how to keep the fire going in the end."

"Did he now? I wasn't aware you two were even talking again. Or were you doing *more* than talking?"

"W-we did a puzzle too."

Amma raised an eyebrow, not appeased by that answer.

"Was it safe for you to walk back?" Alden asked. "It's still pretty slick out there."

"Oh, I have shoes made for this." Amma gestured to her boots.

"Then couldn't you have come back before?" I asked.

"Oh, no. Slush is *much* easier than ice." She waved her hand, but I frowned, wondering if she was telling the whole truth. "But I also didn't mind spending time with a handsome man."

"I have questions," I said.

"So do I. Who wants to answer first?"

"Actually," Alden said, "I think we should figure out if we can get out of here and have a late Christmas party."

Amma pursed her lips but nodded. I let out a sigh of relief. "Well, we did miss the day of. I'll call up Nick and see what he's up to. I hear the city is far clearer."

I nodded, glad it would be her talking to Nick and not me.

"Thank you for cleaning up," Amma said. "It looks better than I left it."

"We were hoping to get out of here today," I replied.

She smiled at us before picking up the phone.

I grabbed Alden and pulled him into the hallway.

"What's the plan for the rest of this?" I asked. "If I see Nick, I might go ahead and kill him."

"That's not usually a good first greeting," he replied. I gave him a flat look. "Stella." He set his hands on my shoulders. "We've been stuck in a house for the last few days and you missed Christmas with your family. Talking to Nick can wait."

"I don't know if I *can* wait. I'm mad just thinking about him."

"And what if it goes south? What if he's angry and the

whole night is ruined? We'll talk to him today, but can we give it until after the party? You were heartbroken after missing Christmas, and you deserve to have fun, even if you're glaring at Nick all night."

I bit my lip. "Okay, I see your point. I do want to enjoy it."

"We'll play it cool."

"Can we even do that?"

"I did it for years. The better question is, can *you* do it?"

I glared. "Keep teasing me and it'll make it very easy."

"Good news," Amma said, walking in. "The city was in better condition than here, and Nick is *very* ready for a party."

"Great," Alden replied, taking a step away from me. "I'll drive."

"Yes," I said. "Please."

I didn't mean for my eyes to linger on him, but they did.

Amma caught it. Her smug grin made me wonder just how much she'd already deduced.

To be safe, I walked to the car *very* far from Alden and sat in the back seat for good measure.

Alden backed out of the driveway, but we slid as he was changing gears.

I tried not to let it show, but I was terrified of getting on the road, and he didn't seem too thrilled either. We veered at every turn, and I couldn't help but glance at him on the way back. His brow was creased with concentration, though he was far calmer than I felt.

If it were me driving, I would have been panicking.

Thankfully, it got easier once we were on the main roads. Snowplows had come through to all the major areas, and Nick lived right off of one.

We pulled into his apartment parking lot half an hour later. The nerves hit as we got out.

I needed to play it cool until we talked to my brother, but I wasn't sure how to. I tried to remember how Alden and I were before, but all that took over my mind was what we had now. We needed to play this well to get through the party and avoid a possible fight while everyone was there.

I, of course, didn't want to fight with Nick—I never did. Sure, we had squabbles like any brother and sister, but there was never a massive, earth-shattering argument.

This could be the day that changed that.

My heart raced as we walked in. But I barely got a glance at my brother before he pulled me into one of the tightest hugs of my life.

My anger dissipated momentarily. He had to be terrified not being able to reach either of us while we were stuck. With Alden there, I'd never been in danger.

"It's so good to see you two." Nick moved away from me and pulled Alden into the same tight hug.

"We're fine, Nick." Alden's voice was soft, but I could hear it shake with nerves.

"Still. All of the reports coming out from people stuck were awful." He shuddered.

"No worry for me?" Amma asked.

"You could keep yourself alive with a match and one pack of food," he said. "And you had a phone."

"Technically, we did too," I reminded him. "We just had to save power."

"I had to distract myself with decorating." He gestured around. "Do you like it? I went all out."

And all out he did, but not in the way I thought he would. Nick had a modern style, and he tried to find that with Christmas decorations. A large, skinny tree was adorned with blue and silver ornaments. After days in Amma's cozy cabin, it felt cold.

"Nick." Amma crossed her arms. "We need to talk about your décor choices."

"What?" he asked. "I think it looks nice."

Amma shook her head. Whatever she was going to say next was blocked out by my parents bursting through the door, both of them pulling Alden and me into tight hugs.

"Oh, thank God," Mom said. "I was so worried."

"We talked on the phone last night," I reminded them.

"It's not the same as seeing you in person."

"I was safe the moment Alden came back for me."

Every head in the room turned. My words hit me right after.

"What do you mean he came *back* for you?" Nick asked. "I thought he was always there."

I glanced at Alden, who looked like a deer in headlights.

Whoops, I shouldn't have mentioned that.

"I kind of kicked him out before I realized how bad it was. He was nice enough to come back. That's all."

"Is that why your truck was gone the whole time?" Amma asked.

"Oh, yeah. It went off the road a mile out. I took it as a sign and ran—"

"Walked," I corrected. "In a very casual, friendly way."

Silence settled over the room.

"Interesting," Amma said. "Isn't that so, Nick?"

"Sure," he said, eyes narrowed.

This was teetering on a conversation that we weren't ready to have. "You said you were going to get some stuff from Reed, right?"

That seemed to distract him. "I did. He's an ass, by the way."

"What did he say this time?"

"He says he still expects the photos you took by next week. The ones you were working on when he proposed."

My eyes narrowed. "Are you serious?"

"Hang on," Alden interjected, "he had you *working* the day he proposed?"

"There were layers to how shitty that day was," I answered and then turned to Nick. "What did you say?"

"I told him you charged a fee for clients who are idiots and he has to pay you double."

"Did he agree?"

"He did. Congrats. Glad you dumped him, though."

"Me too," Alden said darkly. Nick glanced at him with a raised brow, and I knew I needed to get us back on track.

"Can I see the stuff you got?" I asked.

"Yeah. Follow me."

The guest room was filled with boxes, all of which had my name on them. "Oh my God, you got so much."

"He was ready to cut ties."

"I was too. No more bad boyfriends for me."

"Right." His hand tapped on the wall. "Speaking of boyfriends—"

"Actually, Nick," I said all too loudly. "I need to find something in all of these boxes. Mind if I have a minute?"

He blew out a breath. "Fine, but we'll talk later."

"Sure. Of course."

I busied myself with taking stock of everything he had retrieved, trying not to think of all the ways this party could go wrong. Alden and I were not playing it cool at all.

After a few minutes, I finally returned to the living room.

"Hey, kiddo." Dad found me with a smile. "How did Amma's house hold up?"

Dad was usually smothered by the loudness of Amma and Mom. He preferred the quiet, and I hadn't realized how much I valued it like he did until now.

"It did well, even if it sounded haunted with the wind."

"I'm glad Alden came back for you. He's always been a good kid."

"I know. *He* just needs to figure it out."

"He will eventually," Dad said. "Now, get to the kitchen."

"Why?"

"Because I heard you only ate muffins and canned food, and there are fresh vegetables in the kitchen."

My mouth watered. "Oh, hell yes. I'll talk to you later."

I nearly ran to the snacks, desperately needing something other than the prepackaged food I'd had for the last few days. There was a large selection of different fresh things, like grapes, celery, and apples, but I went for the nearest option.

Alden found me shoving carrots into my mouth. "Happy?"

"God, so happy. I was serious when I said I'm never eating a muffin or soup again."

"You're still making my favorite, right?"

"And what do I get out of it?"

His eyes flashed, and I knew the answer.

"Fine," I said. "If you're really good, I'll make chicken and dumplings. I use crescent dough."

"Jesus Christ," he said. "If this weren't a Christmas party, I'd be dragging you off now."

"To have your way with me or for soup?"

"Both. In any order."

I let out a laugh. It was so tempting to reach out and pull him to me, but then I heard footsteps.

"So, now that I have you both, are we gonna talk about this?" We both whirled to see Nick was waiting in the doorframe.

"There's nothing to talk about right now," I said. "Let's enjoy the party."

"You two are getting along really well." He crossed his arms.

"Do you think I can fight with someone who saved my life?" I patted Alden on the shoulder in what I hoped was a friendly way. "I owe him one."

"You could have said thank you and not become . . ." He gestured to us.

My hand slipped back to my side. What did he want to hear from us? That we were together? That we liked each other now?

And would saying that ruin the sliver of Christmas we had left?

"We'll tell you the full story later," Alden said. "Right now, we should focus on Stella's favorite holiday."

Nick raised an eyebrow. "I think we're all a little curious how you went from hating each other to whatever this is."

"And I'm wondering how you stay so annoying," another voice said. "Yet here you are."

I turned to see my best friend leaning against the doorway to the kitchen.

"Winnie?" I asked. "What are you doing here?"

Nick tensed and turned to her. "I didn't know you'd be here so soon."

"You told me to get here at four, dumbass." She tapped the designer watch on her wrist. "Now go somewhere else. I need to catch up with my best friend."

"Remind me why I invited you again?"

"Because you like your sister more than you dislike me."

"Is this what we sounded like?" Alden asked.

"No," I answered. "They have way more years of this than us."

Winnie waved off a grumbling Nick and then turned to me once he'd left. Her lips set into a smile. "So, I hear you two caused quite the commotion."

Alden sighed. "I don't think I can do this again. I'm one wrong move away from fucking up Christmas."

"I'll fill her in. You go explain the ins and outs of fire making to my dad. He'd love to hear that."

"Thank you," Alden muttered as he made his escape. His hand brushed the small of my back as he walked off.

I turned to Winnie, tempted to hug her like I did with everyone else. But she wasn't a hugger. In fact, I hadn't seen her touch the people she dated, much less her friends.

"So, what happened between the two of you? Last I checked, you were supposed to survive—not come back with the life back in your eyes."

"Are you complaining?"

"Fuck no, but I need the story."

I took her to the guest room and shut and locked the door. With how hard Nick was asking questions, I didn't need him barging in while I was explaining.

"It's a lot."

"Let's start with the biggest item on my list. So, are you and Alden a *thing* or . . ."

"We're a thing," I answered. "But we're not telling my family until after the party."

"I have many questions. First of all, how the hell did you forgive him for that message?"

"Not everyone holds onto grudges like you do. You still hate Nick for telling you not to curse back in middle school."

"To be fair, he's done more things to make me dislike him."

They always got on each other's nerves, mostly because they were two firecrackers fighting for dominance whenever they were in the same room.

"Well, I think I'll give you another one." I sighed. "Because we finally talked about why Alden turned me down."

"I fail to see what this has to do with Nick."

"My idiotic brother went off on him for sleeping with me."

Winnie's eyes narrowed dangerously. "Excuse me?"

"Yeah, he told him he wouldn't be friends with Alden if he continued, and Alden didn't want to lose his only friend. Get this, he thought it was *normal* to have to do something so drastic for friends."

"That tracks, considering what his dad did. Did you set him straight?"

"Immediately."

"Good. Now on to the real problem—Nick. Why would he be so protective?"

"Probably the bullying in middle school."

"So? He doesn't *own* you."

"I'm not his biggest fan right now, which I feel bad about, considering he got nearly all of my stuff from Reed."

"Please tell me you're going to talk to him."

"Of course we will."

"Good. He better learn his lesson when you and Alden tell him to fuck off."

"I hope so. We'll be doing it later."

"And I'll listen in on it."

"I don't see you being able to do that without busting into the conversation."

"Hey, I have great self-control. You saw how little I annoyed Nick."

"Oh yeah. And one of these days, you'll be friends with him."

"When pigs fly, Stella." She rolled her eyes. "And by the way, it's good to have you back."

"It's good to *be* back."

"It seems like Alden is good for you."

"I thought you hated him too."

She tilted her head as she considered it. "I thought I did, but when he makes my best friend smile again, I let go of my grudge. Have you heard from the ex that did this?"

"Nick says he wants his photos by next week."

"Come *on*. If I catch Reed out in public, he's a dead man. He might be the only person I hate more than Nick."

"Sorry to interrupt your catch-up," Mom said through the guest door, "but can I come in?"

I opened it up for her. "What's up?"

"We're redecorating the tree and I wanted to see if you'd like to help."

"Why?" Winnie asked. "It looks like a Christmas tree to me."

"Amma says it's the most millennial tree she's ever seen, so we need to redo it with the décor she gave him last year."

"She's very picky," I explained to Winnie, whose eyebrows raised. She worked long hours, and with the exception of our normal Christmas Eve dinner, she didn't celebrate the holiday. "I'll go help. Want to join?"

"Do I get to see Nick get lectured about it?" Winnie asked.

Mom nodded. "She's on a rant right now."

"Yes!" Winnie said before darting out of the room. Mom watched her go before turning to me.

"How long do you think we have until they start dating?"

"Who?" I asked.

"Nick and Winnie."

"Mom, no. *Never.* That won't happen. Nick's seeing someone."

Mom shook her head. "I don't see that working out. She's like Reed was to you—not a good fit."

I would give her that. Nick's girlfriend Cassandra was the polar opposite of him, and not in a good way. She was so quiet that she barely spoke to us when we met her, and she faded into Nick's side like a chameleon. "Even if you're right about that, Winnie wouldn't let it happen."

"What a shame. I think they'd be good for each other. If not *good*, then entertaining. He needs someone to keep him in line."

"Okay, then tell her that."

"Even I'm not that brave." She shook her head and then gestured for me to follow her. "Come on, Stella. Let's go show your older brother how to decorate a tree."

I followed her into the living room, trying to picture Winnie and Nick together. It wasn't impossible. Winnie had dated both men and women, but always from a distance. Nick was always very close with the people he dated. He seemed to love trying to get Cassandra to open up, choosing to talk to her in corners for hours on end.

"I don't care what trends say," Amma was saying to Nick. "Blue and white are *not* Christmas colors."

"It was all Walmart had!"

"You went to Walmart when I gave you legacy Christmas ornaments?"

"I wanted a cohesive theme."

"Nick Summers, Christmas is not cohesive. It's fun!"

"You tell him, Amma!" Winnie cheered.

"Tell me you at least decorated a tree, Winnie."

"Not at my place, but I brought one in for the employees. Everyone brought something from home to have."

"See, this is how you do it."

Nick glared. "Kiss-up."

"Try-hard," she replied.

"Okay," I interjected. "Where are the good ones? We can fix this thing."

"In the cardboard box in the closet."

"You put those beautiful ornaments in a cardboard box?" Amma gasped.

"They were out of ornament boxes!"

"I found them," Dad said, pulling them out. He opened the box. "Man, I remember some of these."

"Which is why it's a crime that he didn't use them." Amma shook her head. "Now, where's the step stool? I want to get these ones from the top off."

"It's back here," Nick said.

"Don't you dare hand that to Amma," I interrupted. "I'll climb."

"Aren't you sore, dear?" Amma asked. "I saw you take quite a few spills in the snow."

"No, actually—" I paused. "Wait, did you *watch* us?"

"Sometimes. Alden, I hope your hip is okay."

The tips of his ears went red. "It's fine."

"Why were you two out in the snow?" Nick asked.

"We had to find *something* to do, and Amma had sleds." I set down the ladder, eager to change the subject. "Now, which ornaments are going?"

"All the blue ones. Then throw them away."

"Hey, I paid good money for those!"

"They're the cheapest plastic you can find. There is no way you paid good money for them."

"Inflation exists, Amma."

"All the more reason to use the ones I gave you."

I laughed at their exchange and plucked a few from the top branches. Winnie worked on the ones at the bottom as she went along with Amma's antics.

I was focused on not falling. But then there was one a few feet away that I leaned for, only for the ladder to lean too.

A pair of hands steadied me.

"Careful," Alden said. He had to have been watching *very* closely to see me nearly fall.

"Good catch," Amma replied. Our eyes had been locked, but I looked at her, only to see a grin on her face. "What do you think, Nick? Was it a good catch?"

"Yeah," he grumbled. "It was."

I could detect his annoyance from across the room.

"Stella, you okay?" Winnie asked.

"Yep, I'm good. I just forgot how to use a ladder

temporarily." I got down and moved it to the right. Alden lingered nearby.

"I'll be sure you don't fall again."

"You do know it's too late for that, right?" My cheeks heated as I said it.

"I have an idea. It's the same for me, you know."

"This is super cute," Winnie said in a low voice. I didn't even notice she'd walked over to us. "But you two are being *so* obvious right now."

"I told you I was about to ruin Christmas," Alden muttered.

"*Nick* is," Winnie corrected. "And I doubt it's the first holiday he's ruined."

"Are you talking about me over there?" Nick called.

"Of course," Winnie said, rolling her eyes. "They were just telling me about one of your childhood Fourth of Julys."

"You told her about the smoke bomb incident?" His eyes were on us.

Winnie laughed. "Nope. *You* just did. I just picked the easiest holiday to mess up and went with it. Now, let me focus on this ugly tree."

"It's not ugly!" Nick defended.

"It definitely is," Amma responded. "Now get back to work."

TWENTY

"You seem to like that corner a lot." Amma's voice made me jump. "Just like you admired the top of the ladder just a few moments ago."

Heat crept up my neck. I should have known Amma would watch where I was looking. I'd tried to keep in check, but there was no avoiding looking at Stella anymore. It had been just she and I for damn near five days, and it wasn't enough.

It never would be enough.

I thought I could play it cool like I did for the last seven years, but now I knew her too well. I'd been sorely wrong.

"What corner?" I hoped playing dumb would help.

"Whichever one Stella is in."

Nope. Amma read right through me. "It's hard to spend several days taking care of someone and then all of that changing."

"Oh, I'm sure. It's also *her*."

"I don't—"

"Don't deny it. You've looked at her for a long time. Do you think I can't see it? I'm old but I'm not blind."

"I'm sorry."

"Sorry?" She laughed. "Ha! Don't be sorry. I think it's a good thing."

"You would be the first."

"Some people used to be protective of her, sure. But you're a good person. Everyone here knows that. You'll treat Stella right."

"You really think that?"

"Yes," she said as if it were obvious. "In fact, it always could have happened, but I'd especially understand if it happened while you were trapped together."

"Good to know."

She leaned in. "*Did* it happen while you were trapped together?"

I almost told her, but then I remembered what I'd asked Stella to do, and it was only fair if I did the same.

"I can't say."

"You have to give an old lady something."

"I need to be sure Stella is cool with what I tell."

"Good answer," she said. "But not the one I wanted."

"Sorry to disappoint. Though I do have to say thank you for talking to me. I know I'm an outsider, and I'd hate to cause a problem."

"An outsider?" Amma scoffed. "Why would you think that?"

"I'm not related to you guys. I'm just a friend of the family."

"Good lord, son. You think after all these years that you're *just* a family friend?"

"I do. Is that wrong?"

"Very much so. Unfortunately for you, there's no getting rid of us now. You're a part of this family, Alden."

"I'm sure I could find a way."

She put a hand on my shoulder. "No, you couldn't. I know you grew up thinking families just up and leave, but they don't. Not us. Not *real* family."

"That's the thing, I'm not real family."

She shook her head. "Blood doesn't matter. It's the heart that does."

"Even if Nick and I fought?"

"Yes, of course. Your dad underestimated what a kind person you are, but we aren't him. We see you."

Overwhelming emotions consumed every inch of my body, leaving me staring blankly at Amma. "I . . . I don't know what to say."

"You don't have to say anything. Just know we're here. You're invited to every family occasion, even if you fight with Stella or Nick."

I gaped at her. I had no idea that she would have been so okay with it.

An old anxiety fully lifted off of me. I wasn't going to lose Amma if this went downhill. It helped more than I could say.

"I don't plan on ever fighting with Stella again."

"Judging by the way you two are acting, I don't think you will either." She patted my shoulder. "Now, I need to go find and torture my son-in-law with conversation. He's been hiding in a corner of his own for far too long."

Amma went to find Chris, leaving me alone. Out of habit, my eyes searched for Stella.

I found her talking to her mom about something. When Melody saw me, she waved me over.

"Alden, I'm so happy you're here on Christmas," she said. "I was just asking Stella where she would live next. You two are friends again, right? I don't have to avoid the two of you?"

"Yeah, we're good." Stella smiled at me. "And there's not much to tell. I don't think I've had a second to think about it. But I really liked being out in the middle of nowhere. I actually feel inspired for once. So maybe something quieter."

"You could be near Redwood Falls! You haven't been, but it's gorgeous."

"I've heard it is." Her eyes slid to me. "I can't wait to go."

"I already said I would show you around." When I glanced at Melody and saw her looking at us with a raised eyebrow, I cleared my throat. "Or you could take Winnie."

"But how will I know all the good spots to get photos? I'm excited not to be stuck with only a Polaroid."

"You had a Polaroid?" Melody asked. "Did you get any good pictures? I would love to see them."

"Let me pick the best ones out, Mom. You know I'm a perfectionist."

"And which ones are appropriate."

Stella laughed awkwardly. "What do you mean?"

"I mean, who knows what could happen when you're stuck in snow." A smile crossed her face, and she'd never looked more like Amma.

Oh boy. How much longer did we have until *everyone* figured it out?

Even Nick seemed to have an idea.

Out of the corner of my eye, I saw him watching us again. Instead of my usual guilt, there was a spark of annoyance.

Stella was a smart woman. Why did it matter so much to him who she dated? Why did he not trust her?

I didn't have siblings, so maybe I didn't get it, but I wasn't a terrible person for her—or at least I didn't think so.

It hit me just how wrong he had been to tell me I couldn't date her all of those years ago, and if he did it again, he'd still be wrong.

I was done suffering in the name of friendship. Love didn't have to come with pain.

"I'm so happy to see you getting along," Melody said. "You two were always so close."

"It just took us getting stuck together to get it right," Stella said, and her eyes went to the Christmas tree. "Oh, geez. Amma is climbing the ladder. Alden, hold my drink."

She shoved it into my hands without another thought.

"Something happened while you were stuck together, didn't it?"

"N-no."

"Okay, whatever you say. I think you'd be cute together, though. I've rooted for you two ever since she insisted she was gonna marry you someday."

My eyes went wide. "When did she say that?"

"It was maybe six months after Nick met you and you started coming by the house more. Of course, both of you were too young then. But I thought that something would happen when she went off to college. Little did I know I'd have to wait."

"So you're fine with us being together?"

"More than fine," she said. "Why wouldn't I be?"

"I . . . I don't know. I guess I thought I wasn't good enough for her."

She gently smacked the back of my head. "Alden Canes, you're a good kid. Don't let anyone tell you any differently."

I rubbed the spot but nodded. My anxiety lifted even further. More people would be on my side than I thought.

After Amma finished the tree, we opened the few presents we did get before the party started to wind down. I hadn't gotten Stella anything, something I regretted now that she was my whole world.

But if things went my way, I'd have plenty more holidays to spoil her on.

Chris offered to let Amma stay with them for the night since the roads were probably already frozen over again, and they lived off of a cleared road.

Then it was just Nick, Stella, Winnie, and me. For a second, it was silent, and Nick finally broke it with the question we'd all been waiting for.

"All right, the Christmas party is over. Can we finally talk about this?" Nick gestured in between Stella and me.

Winnie glared but thankfully kept her mouth shut.

"It depends on how you handle it," Stella said. "Because if you go off on Alden, it might get messy."

Despite knowing that I had people on my side, my body tensed at the possible confrontation. I never thought I'd defy Nick again, and it was terrifying.

Nick blinked. "Go off on Alden? Why would I do that?"

Hang on—*what*?

"Because you did it before," Stella interjected. "And it's why we didn't get along for seven years."

Realization dawned in Nick's eyes. "*Oh*, that."

"'*That*'? Is that all you're calling it?" I asked slowly.

"Er, yeah *That*." He rubbed the back of his neck. "I could call it me being an idiot if it makes you feel better."

"It would make *me* feel better." Winnie's voice broke the silence, and Nick glared at her for only a second before turning back to me.

"Wait a second, so you're not mad this time?" Stella asked.

"No, I'm not. I was wrong back then—I hope you know that. You can date or be with whoever you want."

"And this includes seven years ago, right?" Stella asked, narrowing her eyes.

"Yes, it does," Nick said with a nod. "I overreacted back then and fucked things up between you two. I've been trying to fix it, but you two are the most stubborn people I've ever met."

"Stubborn?" Stella asked.

"Don't turn this on them," Winnie warned. "Stella was heartbroken and Alden was doing what you asked."

"I tried to talk to you about it," Nick said to me.

"You told me to never bring her up again." I crossed my arms to hide my clenched fists. "And I thought *you* bringing it up was a test to see if I was listening."

"I may have been an idiot, but I'm not *that* manip-ulative."

"You do realize how awful Alden's dad was, right?" Stella asked. "Alden's very used to jumping through hoops to keep people around, and you threatened to leave."

Nick closed his eyes and his head hung low. "I didn't think about it like that back then. But now I know I went too far. I'm sorry, Alden."

I wasn't used to apologies. Especially not from people who hurt me. The anger that had flooded me dissipated. "I-it's fine."

"No," Stella cut in. "Don't say it's fine unless it really is."

I looked back at Nick, who nodded. "She's right. What I did wasn't okay, and if you're still mad, I understand."

I didn't know *what* I felt. All I knew is that I expected more anger—not for him to come at this with such regret and understanding.

A heavy silence settled on us, broken only by Winnie.

"Since when are you mature?" she asked incredulously.

"I *am* capable of growth, Winnie," he replied with a sigh.

"But *how*? Therapy? A really good self-help book on empathy?"

"A little of all of it, but I realized that I was in the wrong about a year after it happened. Everyone knew something went south between you two, and Amma asked me if I knew what had happened. When I told her the truth, she went off on me."

"I knew she was a smart woman."

"I tried to apologize but the damage was done," Nick continued. "Alden wouldn't look twice at Stella, and she was five seconds away from yelling at him at every event. I kept inviting you both to things because I hoped you would talk. But Alden is a great listener, apparently."

"I tend to be when I'm threatened with losing a friend."

Nick winced. "Yeah. I would be too."

"I was terrified of even looking at her for *years*."

"You didn't have to be. You and Stella are made for each other. I was too blinded by what I *thought* you should be."

I blew out a breath, the weight of this conversation hitting me. There was no fight. Nick didn't hate me.

And most importantly, I had Stella.

A gentle hand landed on my shoulder.

"Alden?" she asked. "Are you okay?"

"I'm . . . I'm good. Still mad that we wasted so much time" —my eyes moved to Nick—"but thank you for not repeating past mistakes. You realized and admitted you were wrong. Not a lot of people do that."

"You've had a lot of shitty people in your life, Alden. I hate that I was one of them. I had this idea that we were a family but never looked to see what you two were feeling."

"So you were fine with them dating this whole time?" Winnie asked.

"I felt weird about the age gap at first, especially when we were all at different points in our lives. But that's not my decision to make. I should have never stepped in."

"How did you miss the massive crush Stella had on him?"

"I—*Winnie!*" Stella's voice was sharp with embarrassment.

"You were obvious," she replied, rolling her eyes.

"I was blind," Nick said. "I still am sometimes. But Amma set me straight, and we've been trying to get this fixed ever since."

"You didn't even do it in the end," Stella said. "It was a weird twist of fate with the snowstorm."

Nick opened his mouth, but then shut it. "Yeah," he said after a moment, "that whole thing was unplanned."

Stella narrowed her eyes. "It *was* a twist of fate, right?"

"Nick, what did you do?" I asked.

"I may have sent Stella when Amma told me she was asking you to come over."

"You planned this?" Stella nearly yelled.

"Oh my *God*." Winnie's palm pressed to her mouth as she tried not to laugh. "Usually, Nick isn't funny, but this is hilarious. You trapped them together?"

"It was the only way! And it worked," he said. "Look at them!"

I scrubbed a hand over my face, struggling to name the mix of emotions I was feeling. Anger. Hurt. Relief. Happiness.

"We almost killed each other a few times, you know that, right?" Stella asked, shaking her head.

"I'm sure it wasn't fun, but you got there in the end. Everything is good now."

"I'm still mad," I repeated.

"Everything is *mostly* good."

"All right, I have another question," Winnie piped up. "Sure, you're super mature and all now, but you kept glaring over at them all day today. So either you're lying about being okay with it and hiding it terribly, or there's something else we don't know."

"I'm not lying about being okay with them," Nick said quickly.

"So why glare?"

"Um, reasons?"

Winnie arched an eyebrow.

"Wait, she's right. You were being weird today." Stella turned on him too. "Are you lying?"

"He wouldn't apologize if he were lying," I cut in. "That's not his style."

"Something is going on."

"Has anyone ever told you that you notice too much?" Nick asked Winnie.

"Every day. Now answer the question."

"It's nothing serious, but I can't exactly say. I don't want to take away from anything that just happened. Especially my apology. This is a serious moment."

"And you being annoying earlier wasn't serious?"

"It was for something . . . fun. I wasn't actually mad."

"Then what was it?" Stella asked. "Tell me or I'll sic Amma on you."

"Amma started this whole thing, so I doubt she'd be mad. But if you have to know, it was a bet."

"A . . ." Stella's jaw dropped. "You *bet* on us?"

"Yes," Nick said. "And I lost."

Winnie cackled. "Oh, I love it when you lose. Good job, Nick."

"How was I supposed to know they'd get together *during* the snowstorm? I thought it would be after."

"Haven't you ever read a romance novel, loser?"

"Why would you get in on a bet in the first place?" I asked. "You knew how serious it was to me."

"I didn't even realize I was in on it until Amma asked me when it would happen. She's a mastermind, you guys. And I couldn't back out. Both Mom and her would have never let me live it down."

The Summers *were* serious about bets.

"You're ridiculous," I said.

"Does it make you madder?"

I thought about it. "Depends on how much money you lost."

Nick sighed. "Like a thousand dollars."

"Holy shit," Winnie said. "Let me know when the next one is. I need to be in on this."

"No," Nick deadpanned.

"I wasn't asking you, asshole."

"Winnie," Stella said, rubbing her forehead. "Can we try not to start a fight?"

"I've been in Nick's place for hours. I'm due for one."

"You could just leave," he said.

"But then I don't get to see your face when I insult you." She put her hand to her chest in mock sincerity. "It's Christmas, Nick. Let me have something good."

Nick glared in response.

"They're insufferable," I muttered to Stella.

"Literally. At least we weren't this bad."

"Hey," Nick interrupted. "I had to deal with Alden's longing looks at Stella. I deserve to be annoying for a bit."

"You're always annoying," Winnie added.

"Can you just be nice for five seconds?"

They devolved into squabbling, and I finally turned to Stella, gauging her reaction to all of this. She watched her brother and best friend as if they were a bomb a second away from going off, but she didn't look as worried as I felt when we finally told Nick.

It would take time for him and me to fully move past everything that happened, but we were on the right track. Our group was finally back together—as it should be.

We would be okay.

More than okay.

Perfect.

EPILOGUE

REDWOOD FALLS WAS BEAUTIFUL. The front of it was adorned with a baseball field and playgrounds, but I was heading farther in.

I'd never been on a hike. Reed had tried to get me to go, but he approached it purely from a workout standpoint and wanted to find the hardest climbs. I wanted to enjoy it for nature, and thankfully, my new, perfectly amazing boyfriend agreed with me.

Tennessee's normal mild winter returned in January. We waited until a warmer mid-fifties day to meet up at the park. I was nervous but willing to give it one shot, even if I only found a few good spots for photography.

Alden was waiting for me at the front of his chosen trail. He looked good today in his jeans and ranger button-up shirt. The hat, especially, did something for me.

"Hey, babe," I said as I locked my car. "Ready to kill me?"

"This won't be that bad," he said with a smile. "I'm not trying to make you hate this."

"You're getting back at me for the curry still."

His smile fell. "You made that way too spicy."

"I didn't know you were a baby about spice."

Alden rolled his eyes. "Or you have way too high of a tolerance. Now, come on. Let's start this before you chicken out."

We walked along a tree-lined paved path. We passed a few people, most of whom had beautiful dogs that I had to stop and admire. Everyone was friendly and said hello. Many of them knew Alden and asked who I was.

It still made my heart skip a beat whenever he called me his girlfriend. Never in my life did I think this would happen, and it sometimes astounded me.

It had been weeks since the snowstorm. I was still staying with Nick, who had just been sent on a long work trip. They had slowly worked on talking everything out about that night seven years ago. Alden was still recovering from his anger from it, but they were slowly going back to normal.

Alden and I had spent our free time hanging out. And Nick called either him or me every night to catch up. True to his word, he hadn't said a thing about us being together whenever we could, and Alden was slowly seeing that everything was okay.

Nick had laughed when we told him our plan for a

hike, warning me that Alden could go for hours. I'd had plenty of caffeine and electrolyte tabs in hopes of keeping up.

Depending on if this hike killed me, Alden was planning to come back to the city with me to stay the night, and I couldn't be more excited about it. Ever since we had been stuck together, simple hangouts didn't seem to be enough.

One of these days, I was going to ask to move in with him. I couldn't live with Nick forever and I didn't see the point in getting an apartment of my own when I didn't want to spend time by myself. Plus, Nick had already mentioned that Alden was willing to apply to move out of the park and drive in each day.

It was early in our relationship, but where most people went on dates in the delicate days of dating, we threw ourselves into a life together during the snowstorm. Now that it was over, I missed him late at night when I was sleeping alone. And I was pretty sure he missed me too.

As we walked, we talked about our plans for dinner. Alden was addicted to my cooking, and I was happy to finally shed all of the rust and get back to my old level of skill.

After thirty minutes of walking and him trying to convince me to give soup another try, the paved trail came to an end among the trees. "Huh," I said, only mildly out of breath. "That was it?"

Alden laughed. "I may like you, but I don't take it *that* easy on you."

"What do you mean?"

"There's a dirt trail up ahead. That's where we're going."

"Shit," I said. "Is that why you told me to get hiking shoes?"

"Yep." His smile was wicked. "After you, babe."

I rolled my eyes and went first, yelping when his hand landed on my ass. "Is that the only reason you had me go first?"

"Always. Plus, there's a view up ahead you'll want to see."

I wasn't sure what kind of view there could be, but I followed his directions up the hill. I was out of breath when we finally got to the top, and all words left my mind when I turned to see a waterfall below us. My jaw dropped, and I could imagine how many clients I could bring here for photos.

I didn't even hear the voices coming up behind me until Alden's hand landed on my hip. "Come on," he said lowly. "Let's get out of the way."

He pulled me to the side so a couple could get past, but my eyes went back to the waterfall. "This was here the entire time?"

"Yep."

"And I missed it because I was being stubborn about hating you?"

"You have it now," he said. "Come on, we can go farther down."

Alden's hand laced through mine as we descended the trail. The dirt path didn't have stairs but roots that held everything in place. I had to focus on where to step, though I knew Alden wouldn't let me fall while he was nearby.

It was loud near the waterfall's base, but I was so entranced by the beauty of nature that I didn't care. People lingered, taking photos of themselves in front of the perfect scenery. I grabbed Alden to do the same.

"Okay," I said, "I see why people love this."

"There're other views of it, you know. It's two miles back to your car."

"Two miles?"

"It'll go by fast."

"But the paved path is shorter. Give me one good reason to take this dirt one."

"More waterfalls."

"Damn it. You have me there."

"I know," he replied. "Are you ready to finish this up?"

"How much am I going to want to kill you by the end of this?"

"Maybe a five, but I promise to make this worth your while in the end."

"With foot rubs?"

"And other things," he said, leaning in.

"We'll see about that. Lead the way."

He smiled and went ahead. I got payback by smacking his ass as hard as he did mine.

The hike was long and difficult, but we had fun the whole time. We climbed hills and rocks. Though I was tired by the end, it was the most fun I'd had in a while.

And as usual, Alden brought out the best in me.

It was all the more reason to keep him around.

WANT MORE?

Get a free bonus epilogue here!

THANK YOU

If you're still reading this, then thank you for taking a chance on my book. I've always wanted to write a novel centered around my favorite holiday, but I could never manage my time right to get it done.

That being said, I caught the plague (Covid) about halfway through this novel. The plan was to take a break and recover, but I still wrote because I wanted to—something I haven't done in a while. This novel completely took me for a loop. It started as a chore and turned into one of my favorite things. I'm so happy to share it with my readers!

Also, thank you to my editing team, Kasey and Mae. You guys help me craft my dumpster fires into working novels. I can't thank you enough. And to Summer, who made this incredible colorful cover—you're amazing and this is probably the most beautiful book I've ever put out, thanks to you.

And to my IRL support system, Josh, Lizzie, Morgan, and Cass—I love you. Thank you for being with me through my writing endeavors. Whether it be me screaming about my gorgeous new cover, or me telling you the wildest quotes from my book, you're always listening.

ABOUT THE AUTHOR

Elle Rivers writes fun romance books filled with real-world problems wrapped in beautiful, heartwarming happy endings. When not writing, she can be found speed-reading other authors' amazing romance novels, curling up next to any warm object she can find, or singing obnoxiously loud to Taylor Swift.

Elle was born and raised in Nashville, TN, and she considers herself one of the few native Nashvillians who does not like country music. She has eight cats who fight for the spot on her lap, and eight chickens who couldn't care less about her unless she is bringing them food. She lives with her romance-hero of a husband who endlessly supports her writing endeavors, and her son, who is the biggest, but most adorable, distraction.

Made in the USA
Las Vegas, NV
19 December 2024

14969818R00144